THE HUNGER

A COLLECTION OF UTAH HORROR

Cover Art by Carter Reid
www.thezombienation.com

Edited by Johnny Worthen, Callie Stoker,
and Terri Baranowski

A Twisted Tree Press Publication
Salt Lake City, UT
www.TwistedTreePress.com

ISBN 978-0-9990200-2-9 (paperback)
ISBN 978-0-9990200-3-6 (ebook)

CONTENTS

APERITIF

INTRODUCTION

If you've been to one of the wonderful writing conferences throughout Utah, you've probably seen the booth for the Utah chapter of the Horror Writers Association. (In fact, you might be standing at that booth right now, reading this introduction and wondering if you should buy this book. Spoiler alert: you should.)

It's at this booth that I've had the pleasure to meet horror fans from around the state, many of whom are kind enough to chat with me for a bit about their favorite horror stories. And then I try to convince them that if they love reading horror, they should give writing it a try. "It's the only way to satisfy the craving," I tell them.

Horror writers have a tendency to devour horror in all its forms, from books and movies to video games and campfire tales, and even that isn't enough. Like a glutton who gets kicked out of an all-you-can-eat fish fry only to go fishing, a frightened horror writer becomes inspired to put pen to page (or fingers to keyboard). The drive to complete a story can be all-consuming, and once the first draft is done, the author might sit back, pat their belly, and heave a deep sigh of satisfaction.

Then, with a little luck, another horror fan will read that story. Maybe that individual will be satiated by reading alone, or maybe they're a true addict who will be inspired to write something terrifying of their own.

Whichever category you fall into, I hope you enjoy this collection of stories curated and edited by members of the Utah Chapter of the Horror Writers Association. May they satisfy your hunger… for now.

Caryn Larrinaga
Managing Editor, Twisted Tree Press

PART I

ENTRÉE

THE FOOD CHAIN

BY LINDA AAGARD

The cold November wind knifes through his thin windbreaker. Few cars pass this way, fewer still stop for a stranger. He stands on the soft shoulder of the interstate junction, Utah behind him, Wyoming ahead, not a bush or a tree, a house or a store, within fifty miles. Utterly alone in the dark.

He isn't worried.

A black car cuts to a stop beside him, its headlights stabbing the night, tires spitting rocks and gravel in their wake. He smiles as the window opens: a soft, sibilant hiss.

"Where're you headed?" A light, lilting voice calls from the dark interior.

Nowhere, he thinks, but he says, "Cheyenne."

"Hop in."

The interior of the car remains dark as the door swings open, and he can see only the driver, a woman, maybe only a girl by the sound of her voice. He slides into the passenger's seat, feels the warm softness of leather under his fingertips, hears the rich purr of a large, well-oiled engine.

Nice.

Very nice, he amends, looking around him, the interior like the capsule of a spaceship. Colored lights and schematic drawings flash from the console that wraps itself around the driver's seat, giving a glow to the interior he hadn't noticed from the outside. The light reflects on the face of the girl, flashing red, green, violet. She turns to face him, a tentative smile on her lips, a turquoise charm glinting in the cleft of her collarbone.

"Hi," he says.

She can't be more than eighteen, he thinks. Anticipation ripples through him. He is aware of music, a deep, resonant bass that surrounds him in sound, the kind of sound that feels like money.

Daddy's car?

Lucky for him, Daddy isn't around.

"Name's Ricky Lee Brown," he drawls and extends his hand. She looks startled for a moment, then slips her hand in his. Hers is small and cool and dry, as if she'd just washed with a strong soap.

"Glad to meet you, Ricky Lee Brown," she says. Her hand rests in his for a moment, then she draws it back, gently, and jams the car in gear. The big machine muscles onto the asphalt.

He clears his throat, ready to give his line of patter, when she says, "Do you always announce yourself that way? Give people the full sobriquet?"

He whistles. "Sooo-ber-gay? Hey, I'm just a poor boy from southern Utah, girl. Where I'm from, everybody's got three names. But you can call me Ricky Lee. For short."

"All right, Ricky Lee For Short."

He wonders at the teasing, but her eyes, when she turns to him, are earnest, sincere.

"It's just when you said Ricky Lee Brown, it reminded me of a news anchor talking about a criminal. You know how they're always using the full name, like, 'Ricky Lee Brown, the man suspected of the Interstate murders, was arrested today.' Like that, you know."

His stomach tightens for an instant, just a second, really, but a nasty sensation all the same.

He wills himself to relax.

"Never thought of it. You're right, though. Why do you think they do that, anyway?"

"Don't know," she says. "Maybe so all the other Ricky Browns don't sue the TV station for slander."

"Yeah, right. Guess I'd better keep my nose clean then. Wouldn't want all those Ricky Browns havin' a coronary when they hear their name on TV."

He thinks she'll laugh but she doesn't. When he looks over at her, he realizes she's older than he had thought at first. Maybe twenty-two, twenty-five?

"This your car?"

She doesn't answer, but smiles and just keeps looking ahead, the glow from the console lights playing on her features. Not his type, his type running more toward the blowzy blond, big tit variety. Definitely not the type that uses words like "sobriquet." Sobriquet, hell. But she's pretty in a stand-offish way, her long black hair falling across her shoulders like a curtain and slightly tip-tilted, dark eyes that make the crotch of his jeans feel tighter. She'd be like all the others, though. Those cool eyes would start from their sockets in terror, her lips would beg him, stop, please, stop, don't hurt me, don't kill me...

"So, why are you going to Cheyenne?"

He jerks against the seat. In his mind he'd been so close, his hands wrapped around the smooth porcelain skin of her neck, squeezing...

"Just passing through." A line of sweat trickles down his neck. Too soon. He needs to calm down, level out. He wipes his damp forehead with his jacket sleeve.

"So, you've heard about the murders?"

"Hasn't everybody?"

A little thrill of pride tickles his spine.

They grow quiet. Headlights approach, recede. Mileposts come and go. No moon. The feeling he's in a rocket ship hurtling through space comes over him. No more cars pass, no towns beckon with twinkling lights. On I-80 bound for Cheyenne, Wyoming, they might as well be on Mars. He feels the monotony of the miles set in.

"If you're hungry, there's fruit and pop in a cooler behind you," she says.

He turns to her, blinks and rubs his eyes. Jeez, what is wrong with him? Young girl? This woman is at least his age, thirty, maybe even thirty-five.

"Go ahead, help yourself." Her voice is husky, pitched low. He stares at her. Maybe the crazy console lights had fooled him. But how had he mistaken her voice? Gone the light, breathy tones of a girl. This woman sounds as if she swallows ashtrays.

There, his shaky fingers feel the cooler's pebbled surface. He leans down and turns slightly before he's able to pry the lid open. Cans of pop jostle with apples in a sea of crushed ice. He wrenches one of the Coke cans from its plastic necklace, pops the tab, then glances at her over the rim of the can.

Blinks.

Forty-five, if she's a day.

He straightens up so quickly his head bangs the car roof.

Rubbing his eyes, he pulls down the front visor and peers at his own face in the lighted mirror. Nothing is different about him; the same young man he faced in the mirror this morning stares back at him in the glass. No time warp. Had he fallen asleep? Dreamed her youth? To his surprise he feels drowsy. Fatigue pulls at him. Out on the highway, with the cold high desert wind whipping around him, he'd felt great, charged up, alive.

Now, he doesn't feel so good.

With an effort he shakes his head and turns to face the woman beside him. Catches his breath. He is not asleep, and he is not dreaming. Her sagging chin puts him in mind of his mother, dead at fifty.

He places the pop can in the holder beside him, cracks all ten of his knuckles in rapid succession, clears his throat, rubs his Adam's apple. The silence makes him nervous.

"So, do you do this often, pick up hitchhikers?"

"Once in a while." She glances at him, her eyes partly hidden by the folds of her creped skin. He does a quick reassessment. Sixty? For the second time that night, his gut tightens. Time to bail.

By the digital display on the dash and a slight glow to the sky up ahead, he guesses they are approaching Green River. Not a big town, even by Wyoming standards, but it will do.

"It's good you aren't afraid." He affects a yawn, stretches out his legs. "Lots of women are. That Interstate Killer and all." Did her fingers tighten just a little on the steering wheel?

"I can take care of myself," she croaks.

"Hey, I didn't mean you couldn't. But some women aren't so brave." Like his mother. She would never have picked up a stranger, or let one in the door. A lot of good her caution had done her. It wasn't a stranger she should have feared. The day he'd left home—fourteen he'd been—she was making a lemon meringue pie. They'd fought, as usual, and an angry red flood of rage had filled him. He waited, though, waited until she took the golden brown confection from the oven and laid it, oh, so carefully, on the cooling rack before he'd whacked her from behind with his father's ax.

He'd taken the pie with him. Just thinking about his mom makes him hungry.

"Green River's up ahead," he says.

Silence.

Ricky Lee sneaks a glance. The old lady, and she is an old lady, no mistake, looks pretty rough, her gray hair standing out from her head like steel wool, her wrinkled hands with veins like ropes clutching the steering wheel.

He tries again. "What say we get out and stretch our legs, get something to eat?"

"Not now."

Get a grip, he tells himself. No way can a seventy-year-old woman hurt him. But he feels somehow as if he is a mouse, not yet in the trap but helpless, having already smelled the cheese.

Reaching down to his ankle, he pulls a boot knife from its sheath. With a quick, practiced motion he turns and jabs it under her chin, the tip just grazing the skin of her dewlap.

"Pull over, old lady. I won't hurt you if you do what I say." He is surprised to hear his voice crack, as if he's a skinny, pimply adolescent. "Just pull over and let me out."

Her eyes, when she turns to him, are sunk into great hollows, and the look she shoots him makes the blood freeze in his veins.

"No."

"Okay, old lady, I warned you. Let me out, right now, or I'll cut you, I swear I will."

Ricky Lee gestures again with his knife, but he feels ridiculous. A warm wetness spreads between his legs.

"Put your little blade down, Ricky Lee Brown," she rasps. "You aren't going to 'cut me,' as you so quaintly put it. You haven't the strength." She adds, almost kindly, "If you're hungry, get something from the cooler. You'll feel better."

He doesn't want to eat. What he wants is to cry, scream, open his window and yell, to somebody or nobody, to save him. Ludicrous. He has a knife. He outweighs her by fifty pounds and works out. But his hand droops, unable to hold up the heavy blade, his muscles flaccid and weak. He can't concentrate. So sleepy. No longer able to keep his head up, he rests his chin on his chest. The knife makes a soft thud as it falls to the carpeted floor.

The car stops. She leans toward him, a smile on her cracked lips.

———

WYOMING STATE TROOPER MIKE HENSLEY whistles under his breath. Well, if this just don't beat all, he thinks. He wonders what Doc Cartwright, coroner for Sweetwater County, will say about this one.

A rancher feeding stock had spotted the corpse early this morning. He'd seen the crumpled form just off the exit and notified the Highway Patrol. Of course, as soon as Hensley received the call he'd thought of the Interstate Killer. The trooper had never found one of those poor unfortunate victims before, but he knows the MO, every highway patrolman does, and this one fits.

His partner, Jim, comes alongside.

"Hey, Mike, look at this guy's ID. We've got one. I know he looks like he's eighty, but guess what? He's only 31." He pauses, then continues, "And his chest..."

Mike scratches his head. Nothing in his experience has prepared him for the sight of the man's hollowed out cavity. What kind of monster steals his victim's heart and youth and leaves no clues behind?

———

"Where're you headed, cowboy?" A light, lilting voice calls from the interior of the dark car. He can see, even in the fading light, a girl's face and slender body, soft, dewy skin and sparkling eyes.

"Fargo," he drawls, hitching up his pants with his free hand, not believing his luck.

"Hop in," she says, and the car's locks click open.

While half-finished horror and mystery manuscripts lurked in her desk drawers, LINDA AAGARD made her living writing magazine articles and press releases. *The Food Chain* marks her first attempt to bring that hidden fiction out of the shadows. She lives in Draper, Utah, with a daughter and the ghosts of 13 cats.

THE DEVOURING MAW

BY C.R. LANGILLE

Towering mesas of brilliant red stone and stunning vistas greeted them at every turn as they made their drive to the trailhead for the hidden arch known as The Maw. The landscape alone had made the trip worth it for Henry.

Henry's life-long friend, Danny, had insider knowledge of the place, which was supposedly nestled near the top of an old trail that didn't show up on any tourist brochures or guide-maps. How Danny came about this knowledge should have been Henry's first indicator that things were not as they seemed. When questioned about the validity of said arch, Danny would say his sources were legit, and that he had it on good authority that the arch was there. Apparently, these days, hearing something from your brother's girlfriend's great-grandfather who read it in an old journal was considered legit. Henry had his doubts, but he enjoyed hiking enough that it didn't matter if the arch was real or not. Besides, the name of the arch was enough to pique Henry's interest.

It was mid-day when they pulled off the highway and made

the long trek up an unmarked dirt road. It was slow going as the road hadn't been serviced, well, since ever. Deep ruts cut through red clay soil winding around large rocks. After an hour, they arrived at a towering pine, long dead and nothing but a skeleton of sun-blasted wood reaching into the sky like a claw. Hanging from the bare branches were various animal skulls. The blank eye sockets of deer, elk, coyote, and cougar glared back at them.

Danny smiled and slapped the steering wheel. "Just like they said it would be. We're here!"

"This doesn't look like the start of a trail, it looks more like a warning," Henry said.

"What, are ye' yeller?" Danny said doing his best Yosemite Sam impression.

"No, but I'm not stupid. I don't think we should go up there."

"Oh come on, quit shitting your britches and man up. We've come a long way."

"Fine, but when we're being chased down the mountain from some sort of horrible creature, don't be surprised when I slap you with a big heap of 'I told you so.'"

The road ended at the trees, but there was a slight indentation in the dirt marking what looked to be a hiking trail winding up into a narrow canyon. Danny killed the engine and hopped out of the vehicle. Henry followed and was surprised when a cold wind rolled across his face. It was the middle of July in southern Utah, cold winds shouldn't have arrived yet. The skies were clear, so it didn't look like a storm was coming.

The skulls clacked in the tree as the wind moved them, acting as a macabre wind chime. Other than the clacking, the only other sound was the click of the engine cooling. There were no other animals around.

"We follow the trail up, and it should lead us to The Maw. At least, I think it will."

"How far?"

"A couple miles. No big deal."

Sure, no big deal. The hanging skulls made it a big deal. The chilly wind whipping through the trees added to the big deal. The deal was big in Henry's mind. Real big.

Henry's stomach growled, and he realized he hadn't eaten anything since breakfast. He grabbed his daypack from the back of the Tracker and pulled a granola bar from one of the side pockets, devouring it in two big bites. After tightening the straps across his chest and arms, he took a big drink of water from the Camelback hose. It was a little warm but was nice running down his throat.

"Ready?" Danny asked.

Henry nodded and they started up the trail. Before hitting the canyon he cast a quick glance back. All of the skulls in the tree had turned to watch them go, and the sight of all them staring back caused his heart to skip a beat.

"Hey…" Henry said, almost a mumble.

"What?"

The skulls turned in different directions until nothing looked odd at all. It must have been the wind.

"Never mind."

Two hours ticked by, but to Henry it was eons. Each step became harder to take and his stomach hurt he was so hungry. He'd already eaten all of his trail mix and the rest of his granola bars. He stopped for a moment to catch his breath and take a drink of water. The trail paralleled the ridge and gave him a view of the canyon floor below. A lazy stream the color of ruddy mud ran a thousand feet below them. He generally wasn't afraid of heights, but his legs turned wobbly and his vision tunneled.

Henry leaned back so the rough rocks of the mountain scraped his back. The solid surface gave him a small bit of comfort. He focused on his breathing, trying to bring his heart rate back down. As he took deliberate breaths in through his nose and out through his mouth, a squirrel scurried up to his foot and looked up inquisitively.

"Hello little guy, how are you?"

The squirrel cocked its head and scampered up a dead pinion pine. Henry pulled his phone out of his pocket and got the camera ready to snap a picture. His girlfriend would get a kick out of the pic; even though she didn't like hiking or camping, she loved animals.

He focused on the squirrel who stared back at him. The pic was going to be great. Just before he was able to snap it, there was a rush of wind, a blur in front of his camera, and the squirrel was gone.

Henry looked up to see a hawk soaring away with the squirrel wriggling between its talons. It landed up the trail and began to devour the critter. He snapped a pic of the hawk eating and debated whether or not he should send the picture to his girlfriend when he got a signal again. She wouldn't appreciate the humor.

He snapped another pic. Then another. Henry zoomed in as close as he could and found the details came surprisingly clear. The hawk tore into the squirrel's body with a hungry fervor the likes he had never seen before in any nature documentaries. He supposed they wouldn't want to air footage that grisly. The hawk's beak was covered in bits of fur and blood. His stomach complained, reminding him that he needed to eat as well, and for half a moment he wanted the squirrel for himself. Saliva built in his mouth as he thought about tearing the meat from its bones, picking it clean until there was nothing left.

Something grabbed his shoulder and his feet slipped on the trail. He slid to his ass and almost went off the edge, but whatever had him by the shoulder pulled him back to his feet.

"Dude, you okay?" Danny asked.

Henry looked past his friend's wide-eyed expression to the hawk, but it wasn't there. Only the half-eaten corpse of the squirrel was on the rocks.

"Yeah, I'm fine. Just a little vertigo," Henry said.

"Let's keep moving, it can't be much further."

"Okay. Hey, do you have any food?"

Danny fished through his pack and handed Henry a package of jerky. Henry tore the bag open and ripped a piece of the dried meat between his teeth, imagining it was the squirrel. It only made him hungrier.

After another hour and a half, Henry stopped and sat on a large rock. "Hey man, you think we should turn back? The sun will be setting soon and we have no idea how much longer it will be before we get to the arch."

Danny looked at Henry then back up the trail. The trail twisted farther up the mountain with no end in sight. There had been so many switchbacks and curves that if it hadn't been for the sun's position, Henry would have had no idea which way was north.

"No, let's keep going. I mean, say it gets dark. We can continue to push on, or hell, I'm sure we could find a spot flat enough to sleep the night through. You don't have anything you need to be to tomorrow, right?"

"That's not the point, I mean, we're chasing after an arch that may not be real, and I'm starving. I've already eaten all my food, and yours. Let's just go back. I don't even want to see the arch anymore."

Just talking about food made the hunger pangs worse. His stomach roared for sustenance and Henry thought about going back to eat the dead squirrel.

"Come on, we're so close."

"Are we? Do you even know where we are? I'm all for adventure, but enough is enough. I'm headed back."

Henry turned and headed back down the trail. He let out a small smile of victory when Danny's footsteps crunched behind him.

"Fine, have it your way," Danny said.

They started the trek down the mountain, but after another hour they came to a small plateau with a ring of dead pines surrounding it. Henry stopped and his heart started racing.

"What the hell? This wasn't here before," Henry said.

He looked to Danny, but his friend remained silent staring at the trees with a glazed look. Danny opened his mouth to say something, but the words must have gotten lost along the way.

Henry looked back up the trail where they had just come from, but when he did, the world spun, worse than any drunken bender he'd ever experienced. He almost threw up and had to take a knee to keep himself from falling over. When everything stopped spinning, he noticed that was looking down the trail, not up it. Somehow they had gotten spun around and had been going up still, instead of down.

"What in the hell? What in the holy hell?" Henry asked.

"Maybe we took a wrong turn," Danny said, chuckling. "Should have taken a left at Albuquerque."

"Really? You think this is funny? We're lost on a trail that should be easier to navigate than a backcountry road and you're laughing?"

Danny's chuckle turned into a full-on laugh. Henry grabbed him by the backpack straps, ready to throw him to the ground and pummel him.

Rip his flesh and chew on the gristle.

However, when he grabbed him, tears were streaming down Danny's face, cutting muddy paths through the dust on his cheeks. Danny's eyes were wide and bloodshot, and he continued to stare at the ring of trees as if Henry wasn't even there. The man continued to laugh.

Snap the bones, suck out the marrow.

Henry shook Danny hard and the glazed look disappeared from his friend's eyes, replaced with fear.

"Snap the bones…" Danny whispered.

"What? What did you say?"

Danny's brow furrowed. "I didn't say anything."

Henry let him go and crept over to the edge of the plateau. They were above the clouds and he couldn't see the bottom of the canyon anymore. There was a smoky haze around them, blocking out the sun and casting the sky in a brilliant pallet of orange, red, and pink. For a moment, there were two great orbs blazing in the sky, twin suns. Henry wiped the sweat from his brow and blinked away the grime, and the second sun disappeared.

"We shouldn't be here," Henry said.

"No shit, Sherlock."

"No. I mean we shouldn't have come here. There's something terribly wrong with this place. It's as if everything is—I don't know, off a little."

"What are you talking about?" Danny asked.

"Can't you feel it? I can feel it in my—"

Bones... delicious bones.

The temperature dropped and the wind picked up. The clouds overhead roiled and rolled, turning from the brilliant colors to a dark and sickly grey.

"Come on," Henry said.

Danny didn't need any prodding. They'd been caught in mountain storms before and both knew they were serious business. They needed to find cover.

Henry led them up the trail and through the circle of dead trees. There was a flat rock in the middle with odd carvings that looked like runes lining the edges. A rusty stain was splayed across the top of the rock. Henry didn't want to know if it was really blood or not.

Blood. Tasty and salty.

The trail continued up for a quarter mile leading to the mouth of a cave. The storm was getting worse, with lighting inching closer and closer with each flash. Thunder rumbled so loud it shook Henry's core.

"Hurry!" Henry yelled, but his voice was lost in the wind.

As they neared the top, the trail narrowed. There was only room for one of them at a time as the mountain rocks sloped up in a V on either side. The cave opened up before them and Henry wasted no time getting out of the weather. Once inside he turned to find a storm whipping the mountain in a frenzy. The winds blew dust, rocks, and debris every which way and it was hard to see more than a few feet from the entrance.

"Thank god for this cave," Danny said.

"Yeah. Sure," Henry said under his breath.

With the storm blocking the rest of the setting sun, it was impossible to see how far back the cave went, but something told Henry it stretched on forever.

Henry fished his headlamp out of his pack and clicked the light on. The bright LED bulbs flared to life and illuminated the cavern walls.

Old pictographs decorated the walls, depicting all manner of scenes—dozens of different animals, from deer and wolves to elk and bear. Some of the scenes showed mountain lions eating other animals, and what looked to be people. Another scene depicted a strange horned creature that looked like a possible bear with elk antlers attacking a group of humans.

"Henry?"

He moved farther into the cavern, following the pictographs. The scenes became stranger and stranger. The pictographs continued down the wall, showing a drawing of a large stone archway. Through the arch, there were two circles with a fire burning around them. Twin suns.

"Henry?"

Humans hunted animals, piling them up and setting them afire. Horrifying *(delectable)* scenes. They showed people hunting down and eating animals. People eating other people *(the marbled meat is to die for)*.

"Henry!"

There were crude images of men, women, and children being devoured by something. He couldn't tell exactly what it was, but it looked like a mountain with hundreds of mouths, all filled with long teeth.

Vorasker. Devourer.

Danny grabbed Henry by the shoulder and spun him around until Danny's headlamp shined in the eyes.

"What?" Henry asked.

Danny pointed. Near the entrance was a small fire pit with a stack of wood, neatly piled.

"What the hell is up with that?" he asked.

"I don't know," Henry said.

"Why would there be a fire pit and wood ready to go? Who the hell put it there?"

"I don't know. But you'll be damned sure that I won't let it go to waste. I'm freezing my ass off," Henry said.

Before he could move, there was a loud whistle from far back in the cave, followed by a gust of foul-smelling wind.

"What the hell?"

"I don't know," Henry said.

"We need to go."

"We can't, not with the storm outside. Let's just get the fire going, hopefully it will keep the animals away if that's what that was."

They got a fire going easily enough, and soon the warm crackle of flames kept the storm's chill at bay. As the fire swayed, shadows danced across the rock walls, as if the pictographs danced along with them. Hopefully, the storm would blow over soon and they could get the hell off the mountain.

Danny was quiet and sat with his legs curled up to his chest, staring into the fire. Every now and then another whistle would start from back in the cave, followed by another foul blast of wind as if something was dead back there in the dark. Dead and waiting.

Dead and delicious.

As the night wore on, Henry's eyelids grew heavy. The stress of the day and their situation bore down upon him and he found it harder and harder to stay awake.

"Hey man, we should take turns getting some shut-eye. We're going to need our strength in the morning to get back down the trail," Henry said.

Danny's response was a light snoring.

"I guess I'll take first watch."

He took some measure of comfort in Danny's snoring. It was a bit of normal he could latch onto in the sea of crazy. Before too long, Henry's head started to bob. He moved over to wake Danny up to take his turn at the watch when something scraped across the rock in the darkness of the cave.

Henry stopped and listened.

He was about to write it off as nerves and an overactive imagination when it happened again, closer this time.

Henry grabbed Danny's leg and shook it. Danny groaned and kicked out.

"Wake up," Henry said through his teeth.

"Just a bit longer."

Henry punched Danny in the thigh.

"Ow! What the hell, man?"

Henry put a finger to his lips and pointed back into the cave.

"There's something in here with us," Henry whispered.

They listened, but there was nothing but the soft howl of the wind and crackling of the fire.

"Man, you need to get some slee—"

Two steps echoed off the cavern wall.

"Who's there?" Henry asked.

There was another step, followed by something stumbling towards them. Henry tried to click his headlamp on, but his hands were shaking too badly. The steps picked up speed until they were running at them.

Danny scrambled to his feet and Henry tried to get up but fell over backward. He caught a glimpse of something rushing from the darkness. He couldn't see much, but it had a wide-open mouth. The fire blew out as another gust of wind came from within the cave, covering everything in darkness. That's when the screaming started.

Henry woke to find himself laying on the hard ground. It was completely dark and he couldn't see anything other than the red glow from coals. He turned on his headlamp. Danny was gone.

"Danny? Where are you?"

Nothing.

Henry stood, groaning as his body protested the movement. There was a slight sting on his head, and he winced when he reached up and touched the sensitive spot. His hand came away with a bit of blood.

Blood is good. It makes the meat juicy.

"Danny?"

There was no response, but his light caught something reflective deeper in the cave. He made his way there and found Danny's backpack on the ground. It was sitting in a pool of blood.

"Danny!"

A trail of blood led farther back as if someone had been dragged along the floor. Henry followed the trail, using the cavern wall to steady himself.

Henry kept going. He kept his light shining down the cavern, hoping to catch a glimpse of his friend, but it was nothing but rock and darkness.

The whistle came again, along with the rotten stench. This time, it was louder and the smell was stronger. Whatever it was, it was close.

Henry pressed on until he rounded a corner. He had found The Maw.

The cavern opened, exposing a starry sky. Nestled under a rock wall was a massive arch, with stalactites spiraling down from the inside like crooked teeth. A pile of bones and carcasses lay at the base, and the stink of rotten meat hit Henry's nostrils, causing him to retch. The wind picked up from outside and blew through the arch, making the whistling noise that had haunted him before. The closer he got, the more the wind sounded like screaming.

Henry inched his way closer to The Maw—closer to the pile of dead things.

Delicious things.

His stomach rumbled and he couldn't help but drool as his mouth watered. He was hungry. The hunger dominated his thoughts. He wanted meat. Savory, juicy, bloody meat.

The ground trembled under his feet, bouncing stones around the dirt-covered floor and shaking dust from above. As the earth shook, the view from inside the arch shifted, like a television losing a signal. The image skipped from the starry sky to a sun-blasted wasteland with two suns burning hot in the distance. The heat wafted through the arch, warming his skin. The temperature was nice at first, but the closer he got, the more intense it became.

He stood at the base of the bones. They rose high above, dwarfing him. There were animals, but also humans mixed into the mountain of skeletons. Skulls of people long dead grinned back at him with broken teeth and empty sockets. There were other things in the bones as well. Skeletons of great creatures he couldn't recognize with elongated talons, wings, and teeth that still looked razor sharp. Curved horns, similar to a ram, protruded from the skulls. There were tall creatures with no eye sockets at all, yet to Henry, they still stared at him, waiting.

A quiet moan came from the top of the pile.

"Danny?"

The moan became louder.

"I'm coming!"

Coming to devour.

Henry started to climb up the pile. It was hard going as the bones constantly shifted under his weight. He got on all fours and crawled higher when he could no longer walk. Henry reached up, and white-hot pain blazed through his hand as a finger bone snapped. He pulled, but something had ahold of him and any movement caused the pain to burn hotter than before. There was a sickening crunch, and his hand was free. Blood poured from a stump where his index finger should have been. Above him was a bloody skull.

The snapping of thousands of mouths echoed through the cavern. The pile began to shift underneath him and the clacking of jaws became louder.

Danny's moaning escalated into screaming.

Henry scrambled up the pile as the skulls bit him, ripping his clothes and flesh alike with each agonizing inch upward. The heat coming from the arch grew hotter and hotter as he climbed, and his skin began to blister. The pain penetrated throughout his body, causing his eyes to water. He wanted to throw up, and almost did whenever he brushed his finger stump across anything. Each time he hit his hand on a piece of bone, agony flashed up his arm.

He was near the top. Danny lay on bones at the threshold of the arch. He was covered in blood, and his breathing was shallow and ragged.

Marinating.

Henry crested the last skeleton and crawled over to Danny. He reached out and grabbed Danny's hand. His friend's grasp was weak, but at least he was still alive.

"Come on, we're getting out of here," Henry said.

Danny mumbled something, but only a bubble of blood came from his lips. Henry got to his knees and tried to figure out the best way to get them both down without killing themselves. Danny was a mess, covered in dozens of cuts and scrapes.

Tenderized.

His stomach rumbled and the hunger washed over him. The meat on Danny's neck glistened under the weight of the two suns. Henry reached out with a shaky hand. He didn't know how he would stop the bleeding—

—tear the flesh—

—there was so much blood. The air was thick with its coppery scent.

Irresistible.

Henry placed his hands on Danny's chest. He still had a heartbeat, but it was very faint. There was a small cut next to his upper ribcage. Lifeblood seeped from the wound. Henry moved his hand to cover it and let out a chuckle when it poured over his fingers.

He grabbed a flap of Danny's skin and pulled ever so slightly. Danny moaned in pain and tried to slap Henry's hand away, but lacked the strength. Henry, pulled harder, ripping the wound and tearing a morsel of flesh off.

Danny screamed and tried to roll away, but Henry pushed down with his good hand, keeping him in place.

Danny's screamed drowned out as Henry's ears started ringing. The sound became louder until everything else came in muffled. The roaring of his stomach matched the noise in his ears and he couldn't think of anything other than the piece of meat in hand. Blood and gore dripped onto his finger stump, but instead of hurting, it felt… good.

Henry's heart beat faster as he inched the bit of Danny's flesh to his mouth.

Eat it.

He opened his maw and placed the meat onto his tongue. The juices flowed down his throat, warm and nice. He chewed the flesh, savoring each time his teeth ground the meat. Then, he swallowed.

There's more where that came from.

He sighed as a wave of pleasure crashed through his body. Drool rolled down his chin and dripped to the bones beneath him.

Henry looked down to Danny. His friend was sobbing and trying to roll away. Henry grabbed him by the legs and pulled him close. His hand tingled, but the pain was dulled under the euphoria he was feeling.

"Please, don't," Danny croaked.

"Shhh, don't fight it. It will be okay. It will be… delicious."

Henry pulled him closer and bit into Danny's neck. Blood sprayed into Henry's face as his teeth broke through Danny's jugular vein. Danny kicked and fought, but after a few seconds, he lay still.

Henry tore a chunk of flesh off and began to gnaw on it. He

wanted more. Even though his mouth was full, he rushed to pull more meat from Danny's lifeless body.

The bones shifted under his weight. He tried to stand and get away, but his feet were sinking. Something had a hold of his legs. The more he fought to free himself, the tighter the grip became. Then, it jerked him down. He sank to his waist.

Henry screamed and tried to find a handhold, but everything was just loose bones and rock. The thing jerked him again and he sank to his chest.

"No! Help!"

He tried to grab the arch but knocked his finger-stump across a rock. Pain lanced up his arm and he saw stars for a moment. Then, something grabbed his arms and pulled him even farther down. Only his face was above the bones.

He screamed again, then was pulled completely under.

Devoured.

Henry woke at the base of the bone pile. His body was ripped, torn, and bleeding from countless wounds. His vision was blurred and pain unlike he had ever experienced rolled through his broken frame. Something else was inside him. A hunger that overcame all the pain. He wanted to… *needed* to eat, or the pain would only grow worse.

He got to his feet. There was a scent coming from the entrance of the cave, something that smelled *delicious.*

He stumbled toward the scent, sniffing in the darkness, a dog trying to find its buried bone. Henry tripped on a rock and slid to his knees. He crawled, moving closer and closer to his goal.

As he rounded the corner, firelight greeted him. The light stung his eyes, causing them to tear up. The scent was strong and it overtook his senses. He needed to find the source and chew it, rip it, tear it.

Now there were voices coming from the fire. Two shadowy figures sat near it, staring back at him. He could almost taste the meat. Bloody and raw.

He stood, took a step and stumbled. The voices grew excited, but he couldn't understand the words. He tasted their fear though, and it was enough to send him over the edge.

Henry ran toward the pair with his hands outstretched. A wind kicked up behind him blowing out the fire, and for half a second, it looked like one of the shadowy figures was Danny. It didn't matter. Henry was hungry. That's when the screaming started.

C.R. LANGILLE spent many a Saturday afternoon watching monster movies with his mother. It wasn't long before he started crafting nightmares to share with his readers. An avid hunter and amateur survivalist, C.R. Langille incorporates the Utah outdoors in many of his tales. He is an affiliate member of the Horror Writer's Association, a member of the League of Utah Writers, and received his MFA: Writing Popular Fiction from Seton Hill University.

LITTLE RABBIT

BY JONI B. HAWS

Rosa couldn't sleep, but hell, she hated sleep anyway. Tonight she was hemmed in on all sides, her sister, supine and snoring, on her right, their brother on a flimsy bunk above them, and the wall of their cramped cabin to her left. On the other side of that wall, what, trillions of gallons of crushing water? How many feet away from the ocean was she right now? How little drilling would it take to usher in the cold, black death of the sea?

She pulled out one earplug, compressed and reinserted it, hoping for a more stalwart defense against Felicia's snoring.

The ship rocked in the dark, creating an unpleasant pull in her belly. She wished they had a window. She knew there was nothing to see from it right now, but trapped in this coffin-like cabin it was too easy to imagine that perhaps the ship was going down, that they might be trapped in a fleeting air pocket of an already flooded deck. They didn't include panic attacks on the list of amenities in the cruise brochure. The cage around her heart felt like it was shrinking. Rosa fought to control her breathing, told herself her mind was empty.

But it wasn't. Not ever. The meds were helping, but the weight of what the doctor had diagnosed as depression never really left. It hung with sharp hooks from her lungs, chronically pulling her shoulders toward the floor. The nightmares continued, especially the one where she couldn't keep her feet from stepping into the bathroom of her old apartment at Dixie State, the one where she couldn't stop her eyes from staring at Cassie lying in the bathtub, eyelids only half closed, skin pale as bone china in a scarlet soak.

Her throat tightened. The guilt hopped onto its familiar track and began its loop. She pictured herself with Chan and Emily on her bedroom floor, reading Cassie's awful poems out of a ratty notebook.

"'Life is not a thing that grows, but instead a pointless hole,'" she would intone in mock melancholy, drawing bouts of laughter from her friends.

"Oh my gosh, what a spaz," Emily would say. "Pointless hole. There are so many jokes there I don't even know where to start."

"It goes perfectly with the one about her love affair with her bed. 'Only the mattress understands.'"

They had made it through most of Cassie's private thoughts, giggling and wiping at their eyes, before getting bored.

"Your roommate is the weirdest," Chan said, rubbing mascara from beneath her eyes . "I feel sorry for you."

Rosa shot her a headshake-eye-roll combo. "For real. She was okay when she first moved in, but I swear I have never seen anyone mope like that before. Like, I don't know what's wrong with her, but get over it already. Seriously, she's like this giant slug."

A giant slug. Those were the words Rosa had used. A giant slug, like the one in her dreams, poking its head between Cassie's pale lips, a glistening cork, before sliding down the corpse's chin and into the murky, crimson water.

———

"SLEEPING on a boat is so much fun," Felicia said when she woke up.

Their brother, whose mustache looked like a lawn in need of watering, poked his head over the side of the bunk. "Yeah, it's pretty cool." He looked at Rosa. "Thanks for going psycho so Mom would finally take us on a trip, even if we do all have to share this tiny room. Felicia, you snore like a chainsaw."

Rosa's mother stepped out of the bathroom like a bolt of lightning and slapped his head. "Maximus Diego Lopez, you will shut your mouth. Rosa is not psycho. Apologize now, chico." Jacinta had adopted a fencing stance with her toothbrush.

"Ow. Geez, sorry."

Rosa didn't care about Max's words. Hell, she deserved them, and worse. Something had changed in the year since Cassie's death. Dirty jokes aside, Rosa now understood Cassie's sentiment about life being a pointless hole. Rosa couldn't help but feel like everything she did—school, work, even showering, was like a dog's feverish digging at an arbitrary patch of grass. Dig, dig, dig, until the dog stopped and stared at its work, looking confused and let down. What was the purpose? There was none. Only a pointless hole.

"I'm having a croissant and a donut for breakfast," Felicia announced, pulling her fingers through her dark curls.

The movement of the bed shook loose the headache that had been niggling Rosa's temples. She had been visited by Cassie again that night, the slug in her mouth growing into a black squid whose tentacles encompassed her head, snaking around her shoulders and arms, animating them until the dead limbs seemed to be reaching toward Rosa, ready to pull her down into the bathtub with them.

Sleep was not her friend.

"Everybody ready to go in twenty minutes," their mother called from the bathroom. "Let's catch the ferry before it gets too hot. We can find a steel drum band, and Rosa, maybe you will find a fanny pack you like. Wouldn't that be a fun souvenir, mi conejita?"

Wow, she was pulling out the old nickname. Rosa hadn't been little rabbit for a while now. She had always loved her mom's nickname for her. Jacinta used to say that Rosa reminded her of a bunny, because she never seemed to walk, only hop. "So much energy I am tired just watching you," she would say. Where had that energy gone? These days it was all Rosa could do to drag one foot in front of the other.

She sighed, the weight in her chest growing heavier.

———

THE SUNSHINE TURNED the motorboat's wake into sprays of glittering diamonds as they sped toward an island of green palms and white sand. Rosa's long-sleeved tee baked her arms and back while her family members exposed as much skin as possible. Max's trunks rode so low they looked held on by magic.

"Gonna find me some Jamaican honeys," he said to her, waggling his eyebrows.

"Honeys?" Rosa replied. "Who says that?"

"Whatever, Wednesday," he said, switching seats. This was just one of the many stupid names he had taken to calling her as of late.

Rosa sat at the very back of the ferry. Her mother and sister, several seats away, didn't conceal their conversation, perhaps believing the wind was carrying their words out to sea instead of straight to Rosa's ears. Or perhaps they hoped she would hear.

"I just don't know what to do for her," Jacinta told Felicia. "I try to give her time, some space. I know what she saw was terrible, but she says herself they were not best friends. She says she is okay, but does she look okay? No. She looks like a ghost. I feel like my daughter died with that girl."

Felicia nodded with a sober expression, always eager to agree with Jacinta. It made life easier. "Yes, mama, and why won't she put on a bathing suit? We're in the Ca-rib-be-an." She emphasized each syllable of the word to highlight her incredulity.

Rosa kept her head turned toward the water, listening to the engine hitch with each wave it plowed. The wind tore at her hair and clothing.

She had realized Cassie was self-harming when she found the loose razor blades in the bathroom, making sudden sense of the way Cassie constantly balled the sleeves of her baggy sweatshirts in her palms. Initially, concern had needled at Rosa, but then she decided it was more annoying than anything. Good hell, Cassie was such a cliché. If she wanted to carve herself up like a Thanksgiving turkey, that was her choice. Maybe she'd feel better if she tried washing her hair, or letting her skin see the light of day once in a while. She looked like a freaking vampire.

Today the sun warmed Rosa's cheeks, and her own hair was well groomed, but it did no more to quell her compulsions than it would have done for Cassie. She realized that now. A voice inside laughed at the irony, making Rosa want to jump over the side of the boat, sink until the darkness around her matched the darkness inside her. The sunshine felt all wrong.

She tugged at her sleeves and folded her arms. Why do I do this? she asked herself.

Because you deserve it, said the voice. Because you know beauty is a lie and nothing matters. This was the voice of her heart, the one that felt more true than the sun itself. Her arms and torso were covered in scars in various stages of healing. She thought of the blood trapped inside her body, which was itself stuck in the endless cycle of heart to limb, its own pointless hole. She wanted to liberate it from the grind, each drop relieved from the gristmill of the vein. She felt herself crave this even while the tears grew in her eyes.

I hate you! she screamed in her head, and didn't know if she meant the arterial urges, or her own true self.

———

THE BOATMAN CUT the engine as they approached the dock. "Ladies and gentlemen, our ferry schedule will have to be cut short today. The captain of the ship says there is a storm advancing toward this area and projected to hit this afternoon. The last ferry will return to the ship at one p.m."

Rosa waited her turn and allowed herself to be helped onto the dock.

"What do you want to do, conejita?" her mother asked, tucking strands of Rosa's hair behind her ears.

"Um, the beach looks nice," she said.

Jacinta brightened. "Yes, let's sit on the beach."

Max hopped on his toes, reaching down to snag the waistline of his trunks just in time. "Can we find some food first?" he asked.

"You just ate all the pastries on the ship."

"A man's gotta eat."

"It's okay, Mama," Rosa said. "You guys can find some food and maybe some music. I just want to walk by myself for awhile." She didn't know if she could bear the next few hours of her mother's pronounced cheeriness.

Jacinta was clearly reluctant, but finally agreed to split the group if Felicia stayed with Rosa. She pulled two towels from her over-sized bag and shoved one under the arm of each girl. "Meet us here in an hour."

"See you later, freaks and geeks," Max said. He pantomimed a tear falling toward an exaggerated frown.

The beach was littered with kids splashing in the surf while their sunburned parents shouted cursory acknowledgments from their towels. As Rosa and Felicia walked along the concrete footpath, the only natives they saw were a child selling homemade dolls and an old, bent woman, dressed in brights of red and gold, selling sliced mango from a small cart. As the sisters passed the cart they stopped to watch the woman skewer a mango, deftly sheer off the skin, and create vertical slices to resemble the petals of a flower. Her grin as she handed it to the pleased tourist revealed several missing teeth.

Felicia surveyed the sand as the old woman turned back to her cart. The woman froze, cocked her head as if listening to something, and turned to look directly at Rosa, locking eyes. Her grin was replaced by a menacing sneer.

Rosa yelped, pawing at Felicia's arm.

"What is your problem?" her sister asked. When Felicia looked to see what had startled Rosa, the woman had already turned away.

Rosa's heart recovered from its somersault. "I saw a lizard," she said. What was she supposed to say, the mango lady looked at me?

The woman hunched over her fruit, pulling them into neat rows, with no acknowledgment of the girls. Rosa felt stupid.

Felicia found a spot she liked and laid down on her towel, palms up as if beckoning the sun. Rosa planted herself next to her sister, folding her arms around her knees. She watched a young family make a sand castle nearby. Two little boys packed sand from below the water line into pre-molded plastic cups shaped like castle spires. The dad was digging a moat with his hands while mom hunted for shells, handing them to the younger boy to use for decoration.

A wave swept up the shore, reaching onto the dry sand and obliterating the useless moat. Half of the castle fell away as it receded. The older boy shouted, "Oh no!" as the younger began to cry. Another pointless hole. Rosa shook her head.

She found her thoughts pulled back to the strange mango woman, but when she glanced back for a better study, both the woman and her cart were gone.

———

FELICIA WAS ASLEEP, sawing away under her dark glasses. Rosa's butt ached from sitting, so she strolled to the water and stood in the lapping waves, letting the sand whisk away beneath her feet with each pass. The longer she stood still, the farther she sank. Beyond their ship, she watched the line where the ocean and sky met. Sure enough, dark clouds hung on the horizon.

I could just start walking into the water and never turn around.

What about my family?

One way ticket.

Someone would save me.

Take them with you.

Shut up, shut up, shut up!

A sharp pain burned across her ankle, sudden and ferocious. She had fallen on the sand, clutching her leg, before registering she had been stung by a jelly.

"Do you need help, Miss?" an accented voice croaked behind her. The tone skirted on false politeness, like the asker had just caught Rosa spraying graffiti. Rosa looked up to see the mango seller glaring down at her with dark, shining eyes.

Bile threatened in Rosa's gut. "Uh, no, no, I'm fine. Thank you."

"Someone should look at that sting," said the woman, who bent, tapped Rosa's lips, and then yanked her to her feet. Rosa gasped in surprise and tried to pull away, but found the woman's grip like cast iron.

The woman tugged her across the sand, making Rosa trip, but did not let go. What the hell? When Rosa tried to shout she found her voice dead in its box. She tried to draw the attention of others on the beach. Was no one seeing this? Apparently, no one was. The woman was small, but she pulled like a bull and Rosa could do nothing but hobble behind her captor in a silent panic. A distant rumble of thunder escorted them into the dense foliage at the tree line. Rosa looked back before her view of the beach was obscured to see Felicia, unmoved and unaware.

Perhaps thirty minutes later, Rosa was tied to an aluminum chair in a small cinderblock hut. The woman had led her along a path dense with plants, though occasionally Rosa would catch a glimpse of the marketplace through a break in the trees. She had fought heavily in the beginning, but any tug that gained her any ground was quickly reversed by the freakish strength of the woman.

I'm being kidnapped by a superhuman prune, she thought, and focused on memorizing the pattern on the fabric of the woman's bobbing head wrap. She just needed to remain calm until she could catch the woman off guard.

However, once inside what Rosa could only assume was the woman's home, the woman took a length of jute cord from her dress pocket and closed her eyes, touching each of them with the bent loop. Rosa remembered hearing the woman saying a strange word and the next thing she knew she had woken up tied to this chair.

Rosa's tongue was paralyzed in her mouth, but her eyes had no trouble crying.

Through her tears, she saw a wooden cabinet littered with stacks of plastic dishes standing across from her, a small stove and sink just behind. Her fear and confusion overwhelmed the fire in her ankle. How would her mother ever find her here? A few young children stared in from the doorway, bare feet and cotton shorts dusted with dirt. They were the only witnesses from the small group of dwellings who seemed interested.

The old woman crouched in front of Rosa, resting her hands on her thighs. Malevolence shaped her features.

"Do you wish to die?" she asked, covering each consonant with a heavy lid.

The weight in Rosa's chest expanded like a lead balloon. She swayed her head back and forth and sobbed.

One eye, framed in a web of wrinkles, squinted back at her in appraisal. Light drops of rain began tapping the corrugated tin roof.

"Hmph, I guess we will see," she said. Turning to the children in the doorway, she commanded, "Go get me my knife." She padded across the gummy linoleum to a chair matching Rosa's and sat.

Rosa's mind raced, plotting an escape. Her hands were tied at her sides to the frame of the chair, but her legs were unbound. She could easily bolt out the open door, though she didn't know if she could find their trail once she got outside, and the chair would definitely slow her down. She was still thinking when one of the children, no older than five, handed a knife to the woman by its handle. The blade was about six inches long, glinting in the dull light from the single window. The point looked very sharp.

The woman poured water from a plastic pitcher into a bowl and proceeded to wash the knife. Outside, a blanket of white clouds obscured the blue sky, growing ever darker. The rain became more insistent.

Rosa had surely missed the last ferry by now. She knew there was no way Jacinta would return to the ship without her, and tried to let her mind cling to that fact. I'm here, Mama. Maybe she could stall the woman until a search party found her.

Yet, with the woman's back partially turned, this could be her best chance to run.

Does it really matter? asked the voice that echoed within the chambers of her heart. Haven't you been wishing that this game would all end anyway?

Rosa closed her eyes, and watched visions of her death play like movies on a screen. Every scenario carried the common theme—blood. But, relief too. An end to the pain that had been slowly crushing her heart for so many months. She didn't really want to die, but she would welcome an end to that pain. She remained frozen in place.

With the knife clean the woman once again pulled the jute cord from her dress pocket and wrapped it around the blade. Holding the ends onto the wooden handle with her bent fingers, she brought the knife parallel to Rosa's chest, pressing it firmly over her heart.

Rosa's pulse picked up speed. The weight inside churned like the rotors of the ferry's motor.

Lightning flashed, the clap of thunder coming several seconds after. The mud outside shuddered with the fall of raindrops.

The woman spoke a few words Rosa didn't understand, then, looking satisfied, took her knife to the opposite chair and removed the jute, stuffing it back into her pocket. Rosa had not made a sound since she was taken, her inability to speak frightening her more than the fact that she had been kidnapped. This shriveled woman was much more than she appeared. What unknown terrors was she capable of? She glared at the woman in defiance, which brought a wry smile to the old one's lips.

One of the kids sat on the floor just inside the door, but the other had run outside when the rain started. He returned then, grinning and holding a giant slug. It looked like a huge, white maggot undulating in his small hands. Its eye stalks lengthened and squirmed, making Rosa want to vomit.

As she watched in horror, more slugs made their slow journey over the threshold and into the room, wet trails shining behind them. Their pale bodies multiplied, two becoming ten, becoming hundreds, a writhing mass carpeting the floor. Rosa closed her eyes against the onslaught, only to picture Cassie in the bathtub, white slugs popping from her mouth.

The old woman picked up one of the wriggling creatures and carried it to Rosa. "This is very interesting. I ask you again, do you wish to die?"

The voice inside whispered that she was screwed, that she should give in and let the struggle end. It lulled and cajoled, a dissonant whirlwind.

Yet despite the pain, the pointlessness of her life, Rosa realized maybe a dog doesn't dig because the hole matters, but because it simply felt good to dig.

She still wanted to dig.

She stared at the woman, eyes pleading. Her captor wiped a slimy hand across Rosa's mouth, and just like that her tongue was free.

"Please don't kill me. I don't want to die!" Rosa cried.

"Then you know what you must do," the woman said, holding the bloated slug in front of Rosa's face.

Rosa recoiled in disgust. "No! Oh my god, no!"

"I could let you go," said the woman, "but if you go back, if you return to that boat, your life will end as surely as if I were to run my blade through your heart."

The whirlwind in Rosa's chest expanded even further, building until she struggled to breathe.

"You must make your choice now. It does not like where this is going."

The woman cut Rosa's hands from the chair. She placed the writhing creature in Rosa's palm and wrapped her fingers around it.

"Do it now!"

Pain shot through Rosa's chest and she jumped to her feet, fighting for breath.

No, you weak-minded bitch! the voice inside screamed, and this time the sound floated up right out of her open mouth.

The old woman's eyes closed to slits when she heard it. Both children fled. Rosa lifted onto her tiptoes, trying to lengthen herself, make room for the swelling within. She felt a pop, and then another, as her ribs began to fracture. She had no air to scream when she felt razors crawling up her throat, something sharp finding purchase on her tongue.

"Now!" the woman screamed, pushing Rosa's hand, still gripping the slug, toward her face.

Rosa shoved the bloated slug into her mouth until her hand flattened against her lips. Bitter slime coated her tongue as the slug pushed back toward her throat, forcing the sharp thing to retreat. When the gelatinous animal reached the back of Rosa's tongue, its thick body made her gag, and instinctively she swallowed.

The thing inside Rosa screamed as the slug tamped it down, but still she could not breathe. She worked her jaw, hungry for breath, in awe of the pain.She stared wide-eyed as the woman pulled her dress up over her head. Her chest was covered in tallies of dark, ropy scars. Above her left breast was a faded tattoo of a skeleton key.

"Lie down, quickly," she said, helping Rosa to the floor.

Rosa was barely on her back before the woman pulled up her tee and sliced the skin of her sternum down to the bone.

The woman began to sing using tones and intervals unlike anything Rosa had ever heard. She brought the tip of the knife to her tattoo and jabbed it without ceremony, giving the skin a squeeze to encourage a gush of blood. She wiped this with both hands and rubbed them together. Her singing grew louder and Rosa could feel the beast inside shudder, could feel its own fear swirling it into a frenzy. The thing flailed inside her, pounding her with a pain she could have never imagined.

The old woman continued to sing and rub her hands together, the blood first turning tacky, then congealing into something like putty in her crooked fingers. Her song haunted the room, more animal than human. The rolled blood had taken on a solid shape. Rosa knew she was fading and resigned herself to the end, wishing now it would only come quickly.

The woman revealed the object she now held: a small red key—from end to end about the length of a quarter. The key began to glow as the woman's song shifted from a loud, shuddering wail into a diaphanous melody.

Rosa was delirious with pain. The creature screamed through her veins, threatening to burst right through her in *Alien* fashion. Her vision tunneled.

The woman used one hand to hold open the skin of Rosa's chest, and the other to place the tip of the key to the bone as if she were opening a lock.

Rosa had grown still.

The creature gave one last frantic scream as the woman turned the key.

———

Rosa's mind was silent, as vacuous as a cathedral. The storm inside had grown still and, despite the soreness in her ribs, she gulped in air without obstruction.

"You must do this part," said the woman, easing Rosa onto an elbow. Rosa looked down to see light emanating from the key, glowing orange through the surrounding skin.. The light pulsed gently along with her heartbeat. Despite the depth of the cut, there was no blood on her skin or clothes. Though she felt acutely the pain in her ribs, and, oh, yes, her ankle, the key protruding from the bone did not hurt.

The woman took Rosa's hand, guiding her thumb and forefinger to grip the little key. It felt warm, but not hot. Rosa turned the key so that it ran parallel to the line of her body. As soon as she did so, it extruded itself from the bone and came free in her hand. It no longer shone, but looked like the miniature key to some medieval castle, black as ink, the handle worn smooth.

"Where do you want it?" asked the woman.

Rosa winced, trying to sit up. "What do you mean?" she asked between gasps. Her lips were rancid with slime.

The woman lightly tapped her own tattoo and looked at Rosa meaningfully.

Rosa understood. She thought for a moment, then pressed the length of the key to the soft skin of her forearm just past the wrist. The key sank, as though into honey, until the physical shape was replaced by a black tattoo of its replica. Her heart beat wildly, but no longer from fear. She felt fresh, like blue sky after rain.

"Is it gone?" she asked, though she had only just learned that there had been an it, bastardizing her own emotions and using them against her.

"No," the woman said. "It has made you its host, and it is

part of you now. There is no way to remove it without taking your life in the process. It is yours to keep. But—" She raised a finger as she saw the fear jump back into Rosa's face. "It is your prisoner now. You control *it* instead of the other way around. She who holds the key has the power," and she pressed Rosa's tattoo and her own, one with each hand.

"Does that mean it can come out again?" Rosa asked.

"Only if you give it power to do so. Be warned, it will not enjoy being caged. It will always hunger for your suffering, hunger to deceive you. You will hear it enticing you to let it out." The woman pulled her dress on and slid it down her body as she stood. She pulled Rosa gingerly to her feet. Standing beside one another their eyes were level, though the woman had clearly been tall once. She sandwiched Rosa's hand between her own, the wrinkles around her eyes now reminding Rosa of rays flowing from bright stars.

"I will find someone to take you to the hospital," she said.

Tears of relief spilled freely from Rosa's cheeks. "How did you know?" she asked.

"We sense our own. Mine felt yours," said the woman, passing a gesture between their two bosoms. "I still hear it whisper." She cradled Rosa's face in her hands. "And I felt you. I saw a woman I once was in your eyes. Sometimes we find the right person in our path."

Rosa was beyond speech, feeling she might float. She nodded, and allowed herself a bittersweet smile. She said a silent thank you to her mother for making her go on the cruise, to God, or fate, putting this woman in her path. If only Cassie had found someone who recognized the pain in her eyes. If only Rosa had understood.

Most of the slugs were retreating back outside into the moisture, but a few still milled about the floor. The woman released Rosa and extended a hand "I am Sasha, by the way. It was not so nice to meet you."

Rosa chuckled, and winced.

"Rosa," she said

"Stay here. I will get help. We'll get you back to your family."

Sasha stepped through the doorway, careful not to trample any of the straggling slugs. The rain continued to pour in warm sheets outside. Rosa followed delicately to the entrance and watched Sasha toddle through the rain. Just as her savior passed a tall bush, heavy with red berries, a little brown rabbit shot out from beneath it. The rabbit darted across the path, then stopped suddenly and pulled up onto its hind legs, turning its head toward Rosa. It captured her gaze in its own gleaming eyes, whiskers twitching. Rosa's breath caught while the two stared at one another. Could rabbits smile? After a long moment it fell back onto all fours and scurried up behind Sasha, dashing in zig-zags around her feet.

Rosa lifted her chin and laughed. She didn't even mind the pain.

JONI B. HAWS is a Utah mother who carves out her writing time between Do you have any homework and Where are your shoes. She's turned on by a good yarn, both the storytelling and crocheting varieties, and can't resist a good pun. Okay, any pun. She's a sucker for hot baths and cookie butter and has been a frequent host on the Mormon-themed podcast The Cultural Hall. Her first publication was an essay in Utah Reflections, Stories from the Wasatch Front.

ARACHNIVOROUS

BY BETTI AVARI

I can barely move. I know they think they're helping me by doing this, but they're not. I continue to struggle against my restraints out of principle. That's when the spider drops out of the nurse's bouffant.

I freeze, but the nurse doesn't notice the spider or the shift in my body language.

She retrieves the clipboard from my bedside table and leaves.

The deadbolt clanks behind her.

I look towards my feet, but can't see it. Maybe it *isn't* a spider, but if it is, it probably fell into that nurse's tangled web of henna and Aquanet from one of the crabapple trees in the parking lot. I swallow. It's not in its web anymore. It's somewhere in my cell. On my bed.

I hate spiders.

I hate them like I hate public toilets, snot-nosed kids, garbage can flaps, and parking lots covered in loogies. Spiders are just as filthy. They crawl all over everything—dust, dirt, mold, fungus...and psych ward hospital beds.

I can't see it, but I know that it's creeping down by my legs somewhere.

I can't see it. I can't see it, but just like that choking feeling I used to get when I knew the teacher was going to pick on me, I know that it *is* a spider, and I know that it's moving in my direction.

I can't see over my breasts, those tasteless mounds of flesh that developed a few decades ago, turning me from Kiera Knightly to Brigitte Bardot. I miss my clean, straight lines.

Never more than now.

Blowing all the air from my lungs in an effort to deflate my chest, and straining my eyebrows upward, I think I catch a glimpse of black. I flex my toes, and the movement shifts my bedding. Yes, there it is. Smaller than the Goliath I feared, it is nonetheless terrifying. Spindly legs shine in the white fluorescent glow, and a bulging abdomen glistens.

Instinctively, I know. I know that it will make its way up the bed to my face, but I can feel the effects of the medication the nurse gave me. My eyelids are growing heavy, my extremities weak. I don't know how long I can maintain consciousness, but I keep my eyes trained on the sheets in front of my face and will myself to stay awake...

———

MY EYELIDS ARE HEAVY—AND, as I awaken, a faint memory of anxiety tugs on the tendrils of my consciousness.

I know where I am—the psych ward of St. Rose of Lima Hospital. I know why I can't scratch the itch behind my ear—

my arms are tied with restraints to the bedrails. I know why I can't shift my feet—they are also restrained.

I moan and notice a stiffness on one side of my face. Tape?

A bandage.

And now I remember why I can't raise my head—it's filled with a very sick mind which must also be restrained.

All because I was cleaning again. Grout, rings, and bunnies. Of tile, toilet, and dust. Then a spray of drain muck peppered the right side of my face, and suddenly I became the unclean thing. Was that just today?

I remember soap and water. Soap again. Bleach and sponge.

Grout brush.

Bleeding was counterintuitive to cleanliness, so I scrubbed some more.

That's when Ann found me. She'd returned early from the grocery store. Or maybe I'd been scrubbing that long? That look on her face said it all. Revulsion. Pity. Love. Worry. "Mom? Let's get you bandaged up. Okay?"

"But I'm not clean," I blubbered. I hadn't known I was crying. "The drain had a hair clog, and I fished it out. Then the slime, it..."

"I think you got it all, Mom. But you scrubbed a little too hard." I remember staring down at the grout brush, refusing to see my reflection. She was talking gently to me, the way she talked before she brought me here last; like the parent telling their child that a pulled tooth doesn't hurt.

Lies.

But even now I can feel the sticky blood beneath my fingernails... I scrubbed way too hard, and I know it. Guilt surfaces from where it settled the last time this happened.

Tears sting the corners of my eyelids. I didn't want to fight her. Really, I didn't.

I loved Ann—*love* Ann, even now, when she has brought me here, even though she promised me she would never do this to me again. Because I also made promises that I didn't keep.

The buzz of the fluorescent light overhead mingles with another buzz, sporadic but persistent, fading in and out, out and in. In. Out. I furrow my brow and try to focus my blurry vision. There! To the left! A fly, loud and obnoxious. It flies closer to my face as it buzzes round and round; closer and closer the circular routes expand into my bubble. I wonder if a nurse let it in while I slept, or if it found a crack under the door. Flies can fly up high, but they also crawl down low—on discarded fair food in brimming garbage cans, on port-a-potty seats and the piles of putrescence beneath, on dog-droppings baking in the sun at the city park...

I'll never understand that sick hunger.

I blow at it, hoping to scare it away. Instead, my movements seem to have the opposite effect. Now curious, the fly begins buzzing round and round my head in messy circles. I grit my teeth as it lands on my hair. I try to shake it off, but the restraint on my forehead is too tight. Blowing the air from my lungs in quick, short bursts, I manage to shake the bed ever so slightly. The fly buzzes around once more before landing in my hair again.

Flies like putrid things.

Earlier today, when I went a little too far with the brush on my cheek, I hadn't considered the possibility of the drain snake shooting those tiny green wads of horror into my *hair*!

Now my pulse rate really begins to increase. The nurses stripped me of my clothing quite readily, but they didn't give me the chance to shower before they restrained me. Knowing that there's a chance I'm trapped in that filth makes my stomach churn. The thought is all consuming.

I'm crawling in my skin, wondering how I'll ever sanitize my hair from the germs, when I feel it. A sudden movement behind my ear stops my breath. The sensation is so slight, less than a tickle, like a child's whisper during reading time on my classroom rug, but it echoes through my hollow veins. There is no breeze here.

The fly continues to crawl about my hair, from the tip of my crown down to my right temple as the whisper moves up around my ear, steadily, stealthily, until a sudden movement. A lunge. Fresh buzzing erupts, more erratic than before. High pitched.

Frantic.

I flinch. The Valium in my veins made me forget about the spider.

My skin goes clammy and I begin hyperventilating. "Get off!" I scream out. I scream and scream at the top of my lungs in panic-stricken wails; I can't help it! The accumulation of my helplessness and the carnage taking place is too much for my nerves. The spider was behind my ear this whole time?

I'm helpless.

Now it is killing a fly on top of my head, and I'm restrained.

As the buzzing dies off, I look to the door. I've been screaming for help till I'm hoarse, pleading with the little hope left that someone will save me, but Ann doesn't answer my cries. Nobody does.

I'm hopeless.

My screams die off in wails and moans. I bite my lip to stop it from quivering. Nobody is coming to save me. I'm on my own.

On my own, but not alone.

My wrists are throbbing from this latest wrestle; this bed is the tenth degree of hell, and far too crowded.

I try to catch my breath, to quiet my breathing. The buzzing fly has gone quiet, and so must I.

I try to detach myself, to ignore the spider's creeping movements. Usually, when I have panic attacks, I count my number of breaths per minute. With no clock in the room, I count my heartbeats, but they are frantic at best and not a good judge of the passage of time.

Seven hundred and eighty-two heartbeats go by, and I almost bring my breathing back to normal, when I feel a wing fall to my cheek.

Another lands in my lashes.

Gritting my teeth, I try to blink it away, but it sticks to my mascara, so I squeeze my eyes closed. "Stop, please!" I gasp at last.

But that is the wrong request. When it is through, which seems to happen both too quickly and too slowly, the spider creeps back down my face.

I squeeze my eyes and mouth shut and shudder as it crawls down my cheek, especially when its movements are undetectable through my bandage. The tendons in my neck stick out stiffly, my teeth grit in rage and horror. "Get off me!" I hiss. "Get off!"

But the spider doesn't speak my language, and doesn't care to learn. It has claimed its territory, and now it saunters, like a lion to the shade of a tree on the Serengeti, back down to the crevice behind my ear. "Get off!" I scream. "Get off!" But now, fully confident that it can survive here, the spider begins to build a web around my ear. It crawls over my tender folds of cartilage, wraps its spiky legs around my earlobe, again and again and again and again. I descend to deeper and darker madness.

A nurse enters the room, and I try to control my sobbing.

"Get it off me! Please, get it off!" When the nurse raises one eyebrow, I wail, "A spider, in my hair!"

The nurse's badge slaps my cheek as she leans over me. She inspects my bandage, then pulls away with a skeptical expression.

"Don't you see it?" I beg. "Behind my ear!"

I can feel it crouching there, legs pressed against the back of my earlobe, feet gripping the tender flesh of my scalp on the other side.

Through gritted teeth, I hiss, "Please!" Hope springs anew as the nurse leans over me again, but she doesn't pull my ear forward, or shift my hair aside. She probably thinks I'm hallucinating, thinks the bandage on my cheek is messing with me, and thanks to my mop of curls, she can't see the spider, or the web. I should never have gotten a perm. It was easier to take showers three times a day with hair that needed only a little mousse to maintain, but now it's the perfect hiding place.

The nurse leaves, for what I hope is a flashlight. Instead, she returns with an orderly, and a gag is placed in my mouth. A gag?

"How could you?" I wail. "How could—"

A medication is pumped into my IV.

I need help! I need help. I need...

———

MY EYELIDS ARE HEAVY, and as I awaken, a faint memory of anxiety tugs on the tendrils of my consciousness.

I know where I am, the psych ward of St. Rose of Lima Hospital. I know why I can't scratch the itch behind my ear—my arms are tied with restraints to the bedrails. I know why I can't shift my feet—they're restrained, too. So is my head. But the tight, raw sensation at the corners of my mouth is new. I try wetting my lips, but my tongue meets fabric. In a rush, my recent struggle floods my memory. A gag.

The gag.

The spider.

I can feel the cotton candy thickness of the web around my ear; I can't hear the hum of the fluorescent light clearly on that side. I'm not terrified by the fact that the spider has been busy; the Valium is still thick in my system. But where is it now?

My mouth is dry, dry, dry. Due to my crying earlier, my nose is congested, so I've been mouth-breathing in my sleep. My tongue is swollen and feels dry as a cotton ball, but it's difficult to swallow with the gag in between my parched lips. I sigh—and, feeling the rattle in the back of my throat, I try to not wish for ice chips. I smack my tongue against the roof of my mouth and cough.

And feel a jabbing pain in my cheek.

My eyes water and I gasp for air as I try exploring with my tongue. Something small and spindly wiggles.

I freeze. A tear hangs suspended at the corner of my eye.

No

No

No

No no no no no no no no!

Between my cheek and my gums, I begin to feel more

movement, more pain, and I frantically stab my tongue in that direction, but my tongue isn't long enough to reach behind my right molars and into the crease between my cheek. I used to hide my gum up there to keep from getting caught in choir class.

More stabbing, burning pain. I cry out, and my voice vibrates against the gag.

My hands clench into furious fists. This isn't real, I tell myself. This is a lucid dream. Some drug induced—

Sting!

I can't lie to myself. They've fed me to a spider.

I glare at the locked door as hot tears streak down my cheeks and pool in my ears. But the plexiglass window remains empty, no matter my garbled cries for help. I hate these restraints. Hate them! And the gag in my mouth... I don't even have the right to free speech! They wouldn't believe me anyway. They took every freedom away, and left me helpless.

The pain continues to increase until it feels like a dozen fire ants have let loose on my cheek. My wrists and ankles are raw, and my neck is cramping.

I'll never trust them again. I'll never let my guard down enough for them to do this to me again.

Never.

Never.

I grit my teeth. Never!

I have at my disposal a small series of comforts. Legally, I can't be restrained for more than four hours. And I have received one, no, two doses of Valium? That means my time is almost up. They'll release me, if I'm good.

If only I can relax enough to not cause further alarm, the nurses will release me from—another jabbing, stinging sensation interrupts my thoughts; I still can't turn my head, still can't reach the spot with my tongue—I hiss through the gag, if only!

The lights flicker overhead, the hum of equipment white noise quiets before restoring. Moments later, a clap of thunder shakes the outside window.

A brown out. What if the clock resets? What if my name is wiped from their new-aged electronic contraptions and they forget about me?

Sting!

I wish I had more Valium. A double shot. I can't take this anymore. This helplessness, this dread.

Then the spider moves. I close my eyes, steeling my nerves. I'm barely breathing, trying to hold still so that I don't send it scurrying back out of reach. My jaw is slack, and I can feel my tongue convulse, unsure of where to move or how to best avoid contact. The spider wiggles down from between my gums and my cheek, and crawls between my molars.

A new idea crosses my mind, revolting at first, but it may be my only shot. My teeth are my only available weapon.

Can I do this? Can I actually bite it?

Can it be worse than letting it live?

I take a ragged breath, and *chomp!* The spider's legs wiggle, and I can feel it struggle between my molars as I rub them back and forth against each other.

"This is the only way," I tell myself. "The only way."

I pause to check for signs of movement, and when I'm sure it's dead, I try expectorating the pieces.

It's not easy with the gag. I can't purse my lips and spit. My mouth is still horribly dry as I painstakingly dredge the crevices of my molars, and push the bits up and over my gag. It's an all-consuming task, and every piece tastes like the smell of mildew.

I do not wish to inventory every leg; as long as every trace of it is out of me, I will survive.

I will survive and overcome this ordeal, I tell myself. I will be a model citizen, on my best behavior, so that I can get out of this place. And never come back.

Though I'm still confined, though the spider's ground up remains are still making their way down my chin, I feel like this ordeal is at an end. Having gone through all that I have in these short few hours, I feel like I have genuinely accomplished something, and for one brief, shining second, I have hope that it is over.

I TAKE my medications and walk to my therapy appointments listlessly. My cheek still burns and throbs like the day the spider bit me—sometimes worse—and the doctor is concerned about how slow it's healing, so my bandage starts getting changed twice a day. It's even swelling now, as if something is growing inside me. Still, I know to keep my mouth shut about the spider —and, probably because I do, they seem pleased with my mental stability. I call it deception, they call it progress, and they have started to say that I should be out soon.

But I haven't passed every test yet.

If I make eye contact, and answer readily, I earn a check on the right side. But if I look away too often, or for too long, or if I pause to think about my answer for more than three seconds, I get a check on the left side of the clipboard.

"When you're cleaning your house, what are some methods you'll use to stay in control?" The therapist looks up through glasses perched on a thin nose, pen in hand.

I take a deep breath.

"I'll stick to my list. No more than five minutes per task. I won't leave things perfect. I'll leave a crumpled towel on the counter, or the lid off the toothpaste, or leave the spots on the mirror...because messy is still healthy."

"And your hygiene habits?"

"I'll only shower once per day, unless I'm exercising and break a sweat. I'll only wash my hands when I absolutely need to." As I recite this list, I find my voice growing more and more monotonous, until a twinge of pain stabs at my inner cheek, and it pulses. I try to keep my face neutral, and fail. "Just when I handle raw chicken or use the restroom, or wipe my nephew's nose." I feel my nose crinkle involuntarily.

"And what can you do to stop from hurting yourself?"

Another jab of pain. My wound has been swollen for days now, and my eye is almost closed from the inflammation. I've almost gotten used to the stares I get from the other patients.

The therapist repeats the question.

My concentration is broken, and I look down at the floor. I hate this topic most of all. I want to say that I didn't do it on purpose. Explain that if Ann would just clean her drain on a regular basis, I wouldn't need to, and I wouldn't risk contamination. But that answer gets me a checkmark on the left side of the page.

So I stick to the safe answer.

"I'll stop scrubbing every five seconds, and check my skin. If it's red or bleeding, I will stop immediately and put a bandage on it." I look up. The therapist meets my gaze for a long moment, then jots some notes down, and finally checks the left corner. The bad corner. They can tell that I'm only reciting the answers they've given me. I feel guilty for wasting their time.

I won't waste their time, ever again. If I slip, I must do so privately, or I'm bound to let Ann down again. From now on, nobody can ever know what's lurking inside.

I'm a festering wound, but I have it better than other patients. A plump woman in her fifties won't leave her house or open her windows due to her fear of birds. One man is so afraid of defecating that he won't eat; he weighs little more than a hundred pounds and looks like a holocaust victim. I'm reminded at every turn that the horrors of the mind are the worst dictators. They cannot be stopped by means of war or gnashing of teeth. They can only be medicated, forced to sleep but never truly killed. Yes, I have it better than other patients, but I am haunted, too.

Ann comes into my room one day and I stop rubbing the bandage on my cheek. "Mom, are you ready to come home?"

I nod.

The nurse brings a bag into my room. An evidence bag, filled with my possessions. I swallow. This is what I was wearing when it all started. I'm sure that it smells the same— the bleach, the blood, the soap scum.

My stomach rolls. "No!" I gasp. "They're dir—"

I stop myself. What am I saying? The nurse is there, and Ann is looking at me with a worried expression, but I don't want to stay here one more day. Two of the residents have colds, and they sneeze on everything.

I look down at the rubber grips on my hospital socks and will myself to find some composure. But Ann is speaking, rescuing me for once, instead of feeding me to the wolves.

"Are these her things?" Ann is asking. "Were they laundered?"

The nurse opens the bag with a confused expression and

takes a look inside as Ann pulls the nurse out of the room and allows the door to close. Bless that girl! Bless her for caring for me in an hour of need.

Ann returns, and takes me by the hand. "I'll be back, Mom. It's getting late, so I can come in the morning if you'd like."

Anger stirs within me. Is she so easily persuaded to leave me here another night?

"Can I please wear the gown home?" I beg. "We can launder it and return it tomorrow."

Ann looks to the nurse. "Would twenty dollars be enough?"

The nurse smiles at Ann. It's a normal smile, maybe even a bit sympathetic. "No worries. I know you'll return it."

I try to swallow the bile that has built up inside my mouth. It tastes bitter, but I hide my expression as I reach for the bedrail to sit up. I'm going home.

———

AN ORDERLY WAITS with me on the curb as the smell of rain on pavement washes away the stench of iodine and bedpan from my sinuses.

I take another deep breath, and a muscle in my cheek convulses. I press my palm to the bandage as the pain intensifies. It feels like a really mean zit, deep and bulging and pussing—just begging to be squeezed.

Where is Ann? I scan the parking lot for headlights. Perhaps she had to park in the multi-story parking garage. Or she has a dead battery. Either way, she isn't here, and as my pain intensifies, I feel my composure begin to slip. I can't allow the orderly to see me lose control—this is the same orderly that brought in the gag.

My breathing comes quick and shallow as the pain and pressure intensify and I'm hugging my arms around my chest in the cool breeze. Why didn't we wait in the lobby? I practically ran from the doors to get a gulp full of fresh air and now I'm cold, and in a thin hospital gown, with no bra. Damn these miserable breasts! Damn that spider for biting my cheek! For crawling around my head! For existing!

I lean into my hand and moan. The weight of the orderly's stare is urging me to regain my composure, but I can't help it.

I fall to my knees. The orderly is helping me up, but I'm already clawing at my bandage.

He's restraining my arms when I finally bite my cheek, desperately trying to squeeze out whatever infection is festering. It squirts, and my mouth is suddenly filled with a rank ooze. Like mothballs and skunk spray rolled into one, the smell is strong and gag inducing. I spit it out again and again. The orderly is calling for backup, struggling against my adrenaline surge. I'm vomiting all over the concrete now, and the orderly is allowing me to my knees. My knees are slipping in it when I feel movement in my mouth. At first it feels like bubbles, like hydrogen peroxide mouthwash or soda water. I suck my saliva together to spit it out, and gasp in horror at the sight. In a damp puddle in the midst of my vomit, a slew of tiny spiders crawl.

I'm screaming in dismay as Ann pulls up, her headlights illuminating the scene and casting stark shadows. But there are more spiders bubbling out. I can feel them slide from between my gum and inner cheek, down into my mouth cavity where my tongue is trying to spew them out.

And then I'm in a wheelchair, rushed back into the same place I swore I'd never return. Ann is screaming for me, and the orderly is taping my mouth shut.

They think I'm spitting at them. They can't see the spiders squirming in my sputum. The wheelchair bounces side to side as I thrash, but it's no good. My eyes bulge as my mouth continues to fill with spiders.

I know what I have to do. I have to kill them, too. I begin crushing them with my tongue, and they bite me, so I keep my tongue from the roof of my mouth and snap my molars together again and again. The taste is as familiar as it is disgusting, the same putrid flavor their mother shared. But my mouth is filling up, with nowhere for the spiders to go. Until they are coming out my nose.

Choking and coughing in spasms, I can't breathe. My cheek bandage comes off, tugged by the tape over my mouth. Now the spiders are pouring out of the gaping hole in my cheek and across my face, my neck, the gown.

Screams are erupting in the elevator. Ann screams. The orderly screams. A volunteer screams.

None of them know what to do as the spiders cover me alive —until the pain and fear are too great, and I pass out.

———

THREE DAYS LATER, I'm released from the ICU infectious disease unit. Ann has brought fresh clothes. My hair is styled. The wound on my face is finally healing. They believe that my psychotic break was caused by the spider bite, which is mostly true; what matters is I'm going home.

The sun is shining, but I pay it no mind; it never did anything for me anyway. The radio is on, Madonna's *Papa Don't Preach,* and I hate it, but I don't ask to change the station.

Ann kills the engine in the driveway and I climb out of the car —before she can help me. Before I have to say thank you.

A speech therapist is scheduled for the morning. Physically, I'm recovering. But I haven't begun to speak again. Maybe I don't want to.

Ann pauses beside the coat tree, but I turn away from her to remove my shoes and set my medications on the entry table. After a quiet moment, she heads to the office down the hall with my discharge paperwork.

In the corner of the ceiling, by the door, I see a dark spot. A spider. I watch its legs move in tandem as it climbs down the wall from the ceiling. It isn't the same type of spider. No, this spider is hairy and round and brown. As the spider draws closer, I realize that I don't freeze. I don't worry about seeing a spider at all.

Indeed, I'm surprised to notice that I feel something new. Not fear. Not revulsion. Not dread.

What I feel... is hunger.

As an obsessive observationist, BETTI AVARI lives for moments that inspire her writing and believes that art indeed imitates life. Betti admits that she owes much of her perseverance to those that inspire, if not encourage, her growth, and acknowledges that she wouldn't be in this gig if it weren't for the support of The Clandestine Writerhood Guild and the great Stephanie Gittins. Her message for the world is that life is too short to ignore inspiration's call. Regarding horror, she believes in a quote from Edgar Allan Poe: "Words have no power to impress the mind without the exquisite horror of their reality."

LOOKING FOR LOVE

BY C.H. LINDSAY

Varla's pulse beat in time to the bass throbbing over the sound system. Her heels tapped a sharp staccato counterpoint to the music as she entered the secluded bar. In contrast, the butterflies in her stomach were head banging to their own rhythm in response to her nervousness.

A large mirror stood just inside the entryway. She wasn't sure if that was a good or bad sign. Even so, she couldn't help stopping to check the patch of rot behind her ear to make sure it was well concealed. She was using a new homeopathic ointment and had no idea how long—or how well—it would work.

"First time here?" a deep male voice asked from just behind her.

Varla blushed at being caught looking at herself in a mirror. She stole a quick glance at the man. He was tall, well built, dark… and gorgeous. She tried to look casual. "Oh, hi," she stammered. "Yes, this is my first time. Here, I mean. I only heard about it last week."

He grinned, his teeth as perfect as the rest of him. "There

has to be a first time for everything." He held out a hand to her in greeting. "My name's Del. Let me buy you a drink and officially welcome you to The Dead End."

She put her hand in his and hoped it didn't tremble too much. "Varla." She wondered if all neophytes to the club felt the way she did. She'd only been manifesting for a month, and this was her first attempt at socializing with her own kind. Or her new kind. Was it even a kind? It was more of a condition, she thought. Or a plague.

"A pleasure, Varla." He lifted her hand to his lips and gallantly kissed the back of it. "Since this is your first time, might I suggest the house special?"

She took a deep breath and slowly let it out. How many times had Del practiced this smooth charm? Tonight, she decided, she didn't care. "Sure. I'm up for some adventure."

Del grinned and tucked her hand in the crook of his arm as he led her to a small table and helped her to a seat. He ordered their drinks, then sat down next to her. "You said this was your first time here. Mind if I ask how long it's been since you were diagnosed?"

"Four months." Had it only been four months? It seemed like a lifetime. Or was it that she no longer had a lifetime? All because of Bob, her scum of a boyfriend. She'd gone to see him only to be told by the neighbor across the hall that he'd tried to eat the mailman's face and was taken in for testing. The lady told Varla she should be tested, too, because Bob probably had the virus and would have to be put down.

Varla had gone in that day, but not to her regular doctor. She wasn't going to be locked away or put down like a rabid dog if she tested positive. Fortunately, she found a witch doctor who put her on a serum that was supposed to keep her sane and healthy for at least a year—with the exception of an occasional patch of rot.

Del's hand caressed hers, bringing her attention back to him. "The first six months are the hardest. Then you find a certain… pleasure… in living for the moment."

"I'd love a little pleasure," she blurted, then covered her mouth in embarrassment. "I mean…" She was spared a need of trying to explain and making a bigger fool of herself by the arrival of the waiter.

He placed a basket of chips on the table, then a cup of salsa. "And two Dirty Zombies. Let me know if you want refills." He set the drinks in front of them, turned, and walked back to the bar.

"Seriously?" she asked, picking up her drink and looking at it suspiciously. "Why is it a dirty zombie? Why not some other kind of zombie?"

Del chuckled softly. "You'll find out if you come here often enough. Call it an inside joke." He raised his glass to her. "To a fortuitous meeting, and to finding pleasure."

Fortuitous? That wasn't the word she would use. Not when they had yet to find a cure for the virus. Not when her last boyfriend had failed to tell her he was infected. Her anger heated her words. "Having the virus is not fortuitous and I get no pleasure out of it."

Del's free hand covered hers in a gentle caress. "No. Having the virus is not fortuitous, but meeting you is. We can find pleasure in the time we do have. Together."

Del's practiced charm caused the butterflies in Varla's stomach to start raving, but she wasn't ready to let go of her anger over Bob's betrayal. "Why not toast to watching the world burn?"

"The world will burn, in time, my beautiful Varla. Right now, I'd rather meet my demise locked in your arms." His eyes met hers. "To making each other burn." He slowly brought the glass to his lips, his eyes never leaving hers.

Varla's hand shook with the intensity of his gaze, sloshing some of the drink over the side of the glass. If Del could bottle that charm, he'd make a fortune.

She'd come here to forget about the virus and to find companionship. She wouldn't let thoughts of Bob ruin it. She raised her glass and touched it against his. "To burning together." She took a long drink; pleased at the way it burned all the way down her throat.

After the toast, Del stood and held out his hand to her. "I think this is our dance."

Del led her through several intricate turns, always making sure she didn't trip over her own feet. He was an excellent dancer. By the third dance Varla was relaxed and enjoying herself. By the eighth, she was trying a few moves of her own.

When a slow ballad started, Varla didn't hesitate when Del pulled her close. She liked his cologne and was delighted that there was only a hint of rot. It was an encouraging sign that the evening would end well.

They danced, drank, and talked as more people arrived. Dancing became difficult with so many bodies crammed together. The music slowed, the beat continuing to pulse through her veins. Boldly, she let her hands caress his lower back, his tight buttocks. In response, Del's hands cupped her bottom and pulled her tightly against him for a passionate kiss.

For a long moment she forgot they were crammed into the middle of the dance floor. Not until someone bumped into them. She pulled back, embarrassed by her lack of control. She glanced at the other couple, surprised to see that they were making out too. This was not what she'd expected when she came here. "Can we go somewhere else?" she asked. The bass was giving her a headache and the air was so full of the smell of decay and perfume that she was getting lightheaded. "Please."

Del gazed intently down at her and then looked around the crowded dance floor. "I know a place." He grabbed her hand and pulled her back to their table where he left some bills for the waiter. He kissed her again, then led her through the crowds and out the door.

The night was warm with just enough moonlight to show the way. Del kept to side streets and alleyways to avoid people. He only stopped once to lead her into a rose garden. He plucked one dark red blossom, careful to remove the thorns, and slipped it behind her left ear. "A perfect rose for a perfect rose."

Varla caressed his cheek. His words made her heart melt. "You make me feel special."

"You are special, and I want to show you how you make me feel." He pulled her into his arms and kissed her until she felt weak at the knees.

"We'd better go," he said at last. "If I kiss you again, we won't get out of here until dawn, and I'd hate to shock the milkman when he makes his rounds. The poor man is nearly eighty."

Varla giggled, her head spinning with alcohol, dancing, and Del's charm.

He silently led her down the street, up the back stairs of an apartment building and into a dark room. Once the door was locked, he turned on soft accent lights. The room was sparse, with only a couch, a small table, and a chair. Three entryways opened onto other rooms, but they were too dark for her to see where they led.

Del ran a hand through her hair and down her back as he pulled her into his arms. "I know I'm rushing things, but I can't deny what I feel for you. I want to spend as much time as we have left together."

That was what Varla needed to hear. She'd felt so alone since her diagnosis. She came to the club seeking someone to be with; not for a night but until the virus took her reason. A year at least, the witch doctor promised, and right now, she wanted to spend that time with Del.

"Oh, Del," she whispered, not at all sure what to say. She didn't have his silver tongue. "I want that too."

He laughed and spun her around, then pulled her close for another passionate kiss which quickly became more as his hands caressed her.

Varla could think of nothing but the feel of Del pressing against her and her own growing need. Until his manhood shifted and slowly slid down his thigh.

They both froze for several long seconds. Varla pulled out of his arms and looked down, appalled. A fleshy blob sat on the top of his shoe, peering out at her from the cuff of his trousers.

Del slowly bent down, picked up the penis from off his shoe, and stared at it in consternation.

Varla was frustrated to tears, but she also wanted to laugh. The timing was incredibly bad. But she doubted Del would appreciate her laughing right now, even if it was at the situation and not at him.

She put her hand on his arm and smiled. "It's okay. We can watch a movie or something." It wasn't his fault, after all. Maybe they could salvage something out of the evening.

He shook his head. "Next weekend. I should have it fixed by then."

He could get it fixed? That was news to Varla. "I don't mind if we do something else. I like your company."

Del turned to Varla and snapped. "Look, if I'd wanted companionship I would have bought a dog. Come back to the club next Friday and I'll be more than happy to screw your brains out--no pun intended."

Varla's hand dropped to her side. She stared at him, unsure how to respond to this new Del. "But..."

"Look, Darla…"

"Varla."

"Whatever. I don't want to talk and I don't need your pity. If you need satisfaction, go back to the club, I'm sure someone there will still be unattached, or looking for seconds."

Seconds? Varla didn't dare ask what he meant, didn't want to accept what he was saying, didn't want to believe that she'd been manipulated. But she couldn't deny his words, or the look on his face. Or the betrayal she felt.

He walked over to the table as he bounced the lump of flesh in his hand. "Now, if I can find the phone…"

"Find the phone?" Varla looked around. For the first time she noticed that there was nothing in the room to indicate that anyone lived here. She walked into one of the entryways and turned on the light. It was a bathroom. There was a toilet, a shower, and two thin white towels. The cabinet behind the sink was empty of toiletries. Her temper flared as she headed back to the living room. "You don't even live here."

Del scowled. "You're still here?" He brushed past her to check the other side of the room.

"Did you even care about me?" Stupid question. She already

knew the answer, but she couldn't help herself. She felt hurt and betrayed--and more than a little foolish for being so desperate for affection.

Del sighed and turned back to face her. "Look, we both have the virus, we're both going to die sooner rather than later. What's wrong with getting as much pleasure as we can out of the time we have left?"

He had a point, but she didn't like it. "Pleasure comes from more than just sex."

"Pleasure is sex without baggage. I plan on screwing the world before I watch it burn." He coldly appraised her for a long moment. "Never mind about next week. You're too needy. Go find someone who gives a damn."

Varla's temper snapped. "To hell with you." She grabbed his manhood from his hand and threw it at the wall, pleased to see it stick for a moment, then slowly peel off and plop to the ground.

Del watched his penis fall and turned on Varla, grabbing her by the shoulders and shaking her. "Do you have any idea how much that cost? How long it took to get it to work properly? The witch doctor can only fix it so many times."

"Then you shouldn't take advantage of girls like me who want more," Varla hissed. "You, Bob, the witch doctor…" She slapped him as hard as she could. The side of his face sloughed off, leaving rotting muscle and tendon over his jawbone.

His eyes flashed with anger and a touch of madness. "I should eat your face for that! It took weeks to get the muscles to work right, to get the coloring to match, to have it hold up to… what I need it to do. And now I have to start over."

She was sorry about his face. She had no idea he was mostly illusion. Still, she was angry with both of them and needed to get away. She stomped on his foot with one of her stiletto heels and headed for the door. "Tell the witch doctor you want a refund."

Varla was done with men. She wished she'd come to this conclusion before Bob, before Del, before the virus. But if she couldn't go back, she could at least not make the same mistake again. Tomorrow, she'd look for another doctor of alternative medicine. Maybe a voodoo priestess.

She noticed a song blaring from someone's sound system. *Looking for love in all the wrong places. Looking for love in too many faces.*

"Damn straight," she muttered as she slammed the door.

C.H. LINDSAY is primarily a stay-at-home wife and mother. She is also an actress, conrunner, poet and writer. Of late, she spends most of her time being a hermit in her "mom cave" where she writes and runs an online text-based role-playing fleet of sci-fi simulations. She also collects books. Lots and lots of books. She is a member of SFWA, HWA, SFPA, and LUW.

THE PIT AND THE PENDLETON

BY JASMINE ANGELL

"'Be afraid…Be very afraid'," says Lucinda.

Darius has a smug grin on his face. "*The Fly,* 1986."

"How about, 'I'm your biggest fan'?"

"That's beyond easy. Even my editor would know that one. *Misery*, 1990. Try this one: 'Listen to them. The creatures of the night! What music they make.'"

Lucinda narrows her eyes. "*Bram Stoker's Dracula*, 1992."

Matt stands up from his chair and clears his throat. "Can I have everyone's attention for a sec?"

The din of multiple conversations dies down. "We'll start our meeting in about five minutes. I want to wait for a few more people to arrive first. Kelly is bringing the Story-Dice for the writing exercise we'll be doing after we cover member business."

Lucinda turns back to Darius. "This will stump you. 'Do you know where you are, Bartolome? I'll tell you where you are. You are about to enter '"

"What the hell?" says Darius as Kimball pushes past him, shoving him into Lucinda and splashing coffee all over the front of her shirt.

"Aw, come on!" But Kimball was already gone, disappearing out the conference room door.

Setting down the wet tumbler, Darius shakes off his dripping hand and thrusts a box of tissues at Lucinda. "Crap, sorry Luci."

He scans the room and fastens his gaze on Jenna, who'd been conversing with the inconsiderate jerk seconds before the collision. He marches up to her. "What the hell was that all about?"

Jenna shakes her head. "I don't know what happened."

She slides her finger across the screen of her smart phone. "All I did was show him this new app my roommate told me about. It's called The Mirror. The moment he opened it, his face went white and he broke into a sweat. It was gross."

"All because of a stupid app?" Darius asks. "Let me see that."

He snatches the phone from her hands. She crosses her arms. "Be my guest," she says.

Darius pushes the 'Start' button and a white dot appears at the center of the black screen. He peers closer to it, squinting and the dot grows larger. It evolves into a black and white spiral like those found on hypnotic glasses. His vision narrows and darkness consumes the room.

He blinks once, then twice.

"Very funny. Nice try, Jenna. You can turn the lights on now."

The putrid odor of hydrogen sulfide invades his nostrils and he nearly wretches. His stomach turns at the stench. It's like a mixture of decay, brine fly larvae, and bacteria. The kind of stink that came from the Great Salt Lake but it wasn't the time of year for that.

He swallows and his throat protests as if he's swallowing a lump of wool rather than saliva. His temples pulse, pressure builds in his sinuses and blood rushes to his head. Gravity doesn't feel right, pulling him in wrong directions. He turns his head to orient himself but his whole body sways. There's a sound of creaking ropes echoing off stone walls.

He shakes his head. It had to be virtual reality. It was exactly like the times he'd used his brother's high-end VR set. He reaches for the goggles on his face but he finds his hands immobile, bound flat against his sides. He struggles against the ropes restraining his hands and he manages to free one, then the other.

He feels for the VR headset but none of the familiar plastic greets him. No tether or high tech gear. No goggles to shake off. He gropes frantically but to no avail.

His abdomen clenches and the pounding of blood rushing to his head compounds. He sucks in the muggy air, his lungs pumping quickly. He realizes there is nothing virtual about this reality.

A chilling draft slithers across his face and his skin breaks out into gooseflesh. He peers into the darkness.

"Hello?" He tastes the humid mildew odor hanging in the stifling air. "Is anyone there?"

His voice ricochets off something like a cavern, damp and enormous. His insides tighten. His breathing increases.

The immensity of the cavern recalls a trip he took once to the Homestead Crater in Midway. He'd gone with his family to see the underground hot springs the summer before second grade. This is no crater though; it lacks the hole at the top.

The thick stench in the humid air indicates a geothermal spring.

A gnawing stirs in his abdomen. It is not a physical hunger, but a dull need for something—something yet unnamable.

Drip-drip-splat.

He flinches, squeezing his eyes shut to protect from something viscous and cold—like jelly chilled from the refrigerator—sliding down his forehead and into his hair. He turns his head after another piece of what could possibly be the Blob splatters his chin and makes a snail trail to his left ear.

He opens his eyes and sees the outline of his body showing stark against the pitch black cavern. A faint glow below reveals a thick chain the size of a large intestine wrapped around his ankles, suspending him from above. He arches his neck and sees light flickering like a desolate candle below him, impossibly far below.

Above, the minuscule light gives him just enough visibility to see the ceiling he hangs from heave and undulate like an angry sea. Tiny black Boxelder beetles with reddish-orange markings march down the legs of his jeans toward his torso. He recalls seeing those six-legged pests erupting like a fountain from a young tree he'd trimmed last fall.

He wriggles in desperation and the Boxelder bugs fall past him and fly off.

The small black and red insects are replaced by larger, all-black ones which cling to his neck and face. Beetles, but not ones he has seen up close. His skin grows damp where they crawl. He flinches as they sting his skin.

Blister beetles.

A blister beetle swarm—the way his childhood friend had died after falling down a ravine on a hike in Mill Creek Canyon.

The toxin irritates the skin until blisters form and the victim's airway closes.

Darius pulls his torso into a sit-up and violently swings his head back. The force yanks his body backward, his spine protesting with a sharp twinge he instantly laments but the beetles fly away.

A split second of relief is overshadowed with a resurgence of panic. His eyes grow wide at the even larger, flat brown papery insects scurrying down his pant legs now. One drops onto his chin and hisses at him, the tiny legs scurrying across his jawline. He releases a manly shriek and then regrets opening his mouth when another moves dangerously close to his lips.

He swats at his face, gags and spits—shrieks again and shudders in disgust. Memories of placing his hand under the bathroom faucet of his Sugarhouse apartment and two roaches splashing onto his fingers compounds the agony.

Darius's stomach lurches suddenly, the feeling of an elevator dropping before the occupants are ready for it to move. All remaining bugs tumble off.

Metal clinks on metal overhead and his body sways, descending toward the faint light below. He arches his neck back, straining to glimpse his fate until the muscles in his shoulders revolt and he relaxes limp and pendulous.

A bone-chilling howl spirits up the cavern and every hair on his body stands upright. The primordial survival instinct innate in all living creatures electrifies his senses.

He folds in on himself, hands groping for the chains binding his ankles but his body gives out—lungs burning with exertion —and he unfolds, swaying back and forth. The chains hold him with unforgiving metal certainty.

His head pounds, so full of blood, his eyeballs too heavy as if Godzilla is balancing his weight between them. The terrible insect-covered ceiling disappears from view and the clinking of the chains taking him farther down reverberates against the narrowing cavern walls.

He rues the moment he untied his hands for now his arms hang uncomfortably past his head and shoulders. Yet nothing compares to the hollow sensation in the pit of his stomach. The abyss inside him like a feral animal, gnawing, seeking that which it can't have. Now growing in urgency and intensity, the sensation upstages the blisters forming on his face and the ill-effects gravity continues inflicting upon his swaying body.

The cavern narrows, the dripping rock walls close in on him deftly, gradually. The walls exhibit movement but not like the cavern ceiling. Clothed in darkness, hidden, sinister shapes protrude and vanish.

The chains clutching his body in their iron grasp ominously lower him ever closer to his subterranean fate and the owner of the bowel-churning howl.

Darius sways back and forth, closer to the curved walls. He swings near a short ledge where three figures with vacant stares amble toward him. His eyes widen and he recoils as the undead stretch their arms for him—strings of putrid skin dangling from their skeletal forms.

Intensified moans and death rattles vibrate out of their slack jaws that drip with rancid black bile. They bite the air in expectation, so eager to fill the emptiness within.

Darius cringes, bracing for impact and uses his arms to protect his face from the inevitable onslaught. One zombie grabs hold of the sleeve of his t-shirt and the others dive headlong from the ledge like dominos in a row.

Darius cries out—his scream deep and primeval, realizing

two of the undead dangle from his shoulder while the other has fallen to the depths below. A string of obscenities fly from his lips as the zombie's skeletal fingers dig deep into his flesh.

The second zombie climbs up the first one's body like a ladder, shoving its head off its shoulders in its frenzy to reach Darius. The decaying skull plummets into the pit, jaws still chomping at the air.

With one arm bent against his chest, Darius pries a putrid finger from his throbbing shoulder. With equal effort, he pries a second before the zombie lunges at his face. White streaks of terror blind Darius and he whips his head around. The zombie's teeth graze the side of his skull and Darius's black hair snags between its fetid teeth.

The zombie scratches his collar bones, grasping for a hand hold and Darius wriggles frantically, the reeking stench of decay nearly choking him. The loathsome jaws snap again, this time bearing down on the tip of Darius's ear where the cartilage separates from the meat.

Darius screams in pain, peels the final finger from his shoulder, and flings the zombie off him. The body of the first zombie plunges with the second to meet the third along with a piece of Darius's ear and his hair lodged between the zombie's teeth.

The remains of his ear burns as do the ruts carved across his collarbones. He curls in on himself wondering about the infection rate of the zombie virus.

The unnamable hole in his insides intensifies. Insatiable, aching, and gluttonous. Outshining the discomforts of his physical body. A maniacal demand for flesh and blood, and the gooey stuff mixed in, spears his psyche. His mind and body cry out and consciousness fades away.

Darius comes to with a start, woken by a soul-wrenching

sound. Every hair on his neck stands at attention and his heart beats painfully in his chest.

The howl. Mournful with longing and promising death.

Swinging to and fro, he is delivered ever closer to the walls of the cavern—ever descending—swallowed whole by the immense pit.

A set of bright golden eyes stares back at him from the shadows. He wrenches his head around, his breaths desperate and straining.

The golden stare appears and fastens itself on his throat.

It is real.

From a short ledge, quivering lips reveal yellowed canines dripping with saliva. They lunge and snap mere inches from Darius's face. Spittle sprays across him and foul breath—hot and sickening—rushes forth. A blur of brown fur, frothy with sweat leaps at him.

The rattle of chains mingle with the unforgiving snarling. Five knife-like claws lacerate Darius's chest, raking red furrows across his skin. His scream echoes through the cavern, the wounds light up like an airport runway. His lungs seize—paralyzed, one second, two seconds—before restarting with a desperate gasp and he swings away.

It is only a moment of respite; there will come the inevitable swing back towards the ledge. Every muscle in his body is taunt with anticipation, replete with the horror of what awaits.

No foul breath, no scythe-like claws, no savagery. He swings in and swings away—seeking, searching for the golden gaze yet only blackness answers back.

With each heave of his lungs, blood from the ruts in his chest stream down his neck, pooling in his ears. The adrenaline rocketing through his veins will not allow his breathing to slow despite the pain.

Minutes pass and disbelief gives way to relief. He gasps for breath, his mind racing, wondering if lycanthropy trumps zombie virus.

The ravenous yearning within rises up, overshadowing all previous concerns. The hollow ache, demanding and insistent, pulses inside. A voracious desire, visceral and seeking. For freedom, for the night, for fangs sunk deep in hot flesh.

The glow of warm light below becomes brighter and Darius descends ever closer to its source.

The run-in with the Wolf Man left him spinning to the left and then to the right, unwinding with each arc across the heavy air of the cavern.

Descending farther down, down, down.

He glimpses a visage of mismatched features—stitches and scars across cadaver's skin and Darius recoils at the coming assault. Mismatched eyes, one light blue and the other brown, reflect an impossible mix of fury and melancholy. With inhuman strength, a meaty hand grasps his right arm, the sensation like a blood pressure cuff squeezing too tight. A terrible pop reverberates through Darius before he's unceremoniously released.

He cries out—the pain exploding from his dislocated shoulder nearly unbearable.

He is marked by Frankenstein's Creature. His favorite monster by far. A line from Mary Shelley's *Frankenstein* takes flight in his mind, "I have love in me the likes of which you can scarcely imagine and rage the likes of which you would not believe."

He holds his breath and waits for the creature to finish him, to rip his arm from his body, but it never comes. Only the inevitable burgeoning need, the gripping desire, the yearning in the hollows of his body radiates nearly choking him with its intensity. The hunger grows.

He opens his eyes and a shadow flitters across Darius's face, stretching, elongating, inhuman. All senses on alert, he dares not to breathe.

Shadows splash across the walls. One catches his eye, a darkness in the shape of a tree branch reaching across, tipped with five smaller branches like elongated fingers with claw-like nails.

Darius scans the hidden ledges from where the monsters emerge.

There. Stark white in contrast to the jet black cavern. Its ghastly visage with rat-like features, bat ears and haunting eyes glowing with an eerie inner flame.

The cinematic predecessor to Dracula, Count Orlok, the Nosferatu. Nourished on death.

Without warning, the Count leaps upon Darius and perches on his torso with the ease of a nocturnal animal. He leans in toward Darius's throat. Grains of dirt tumble from the count's coat. The scent of earth from the graveyards of the Black Death fills the air. His white lips peel back revealing fangs like a rodent's, large and protruding, readying to sink them into the tender flesh of Darius's neck.

The sounds of noxious slurping fills his ears.

The count leaps away in a flash of shadow and Darius's heartbeat slows, tentative for the first time since being in the pit as if it is unsure if there is enough blood to continue pumping. Weakness floods over him and his head spins.

Like a wraith possessing him from within, its desire colors

everything, seeks to exert its will, plunging into a bottomless pit of longing and desire. Vacant, never full, the craving over-whelming. Blood, life, human connection.

Thoughts in Darius's mind stumble around as if in a fog. His beloved monsters. He knows each one intimately, each starring in his published stories. He'd taken them and harnessed their power with his pen. His words their prison for his exploitation—the classic monsters reimagined. Made to do his bidding.

Now he dangles at their mercy, being eaten alive with their ageless yearning.

Darius swings back and forth, the light below visible like never before. Thoughts form like ghosts, coalescing and fading. He swings toward human legs and bare feet standing on a ledge. An attractive female clad in hot pink yoga apparel seems oddly suspect.

A faint inkling of familiarity flares in Darius's mind.

The next swing brings him closer to the tan, blue-eyed, perfectly–styled blonde woman sporting a smile of unnaturally white teeth.

Yvonne Wexler. His stalker ex-girlfriend from Utah State. She holds up a pair of fuzzy, leopard-print handcuffs. "You're my one and only. You're my one and only."

No monster could compare, none chilled his blood like the face of Yvonne Wexler. He broke into a new cold sweat. He could still smell the trunk of the car where she'd imprisoned him for three days. It still had that unmistakable new car scent.

She'd drugged his water bottle during baseball practice and locked him in the trunk of her parent's Lincoln. His airway had nearly closed up due to all the cat dander trapped in there with him. Her family showed prize Himalayan cats and must have stored their equipment in the trunk.

The mailman heard his pounding and he spent nearly a week in the hospital on albuterol treatments after the paramedics arrived. Daddy's girl, spoiled rotten, always gets what she wants, and Darius had been no exception. At least until the restraining order.

He'd rather die at the hands of any of those others—but not Yvonne's. Anyone but her.

A handcuff clinks ominously around his wrist, squeezing too tight, crunching the bone amid sounds of fracturing.

"You're my one and only." Her voice rings in his ears, he squeezes his eyes shut.

The emptiness hits him like a sledgehammer. Yearning, grasping, never satisfied. Deep inside him, the void within his stalker mingles with that of the monsters before her. Hungry for control, demanding, ever-seeking, unfulfilled. A vacuous chasm of dissatisfaction and want.

Tentatively, he opens his eyes and a sight he doesn't expect wavers below him.

A circle of flaming torches flicker and dance above the surface of water so still it's like a mirror of smooth obsidian.

Darius is suspended several feet over the water. He catches his reflection and hardly recognizes the man staring back. Images of those who'd marked him during his descent into the pit superimpose over his weary features. Each wound on his body a story, a reminder of the need within.

A ripple travels over the still surface as the sound of a mechanism comes to life. The water level recedes and sluices off a circular slab of rock, revealing a bound figure—a man lying on his back with a sack concealing his head. The moat of stygian waters gives way to the writhing bodies of the monsters that had marked Darius. Along with other creatures of the night, they encircle the man on the slab in a hideous frenzy.

Darius cranes his neck toward the captive figure. Expensive shoes adorn his feet to match his custom-tailored suit, shiny watch, and wedding ring on his finger. Between his hands he grasps a shining crystal trophy and the engraving beckons Darius's gaze.

The coveted Exemplary Author award.

The man wriggles against his restraints and the emptiness inside Darius flares like a forest fire. The walls of the pit glow and heat radiates with menacing fervor.

An unseen force yanks Darius's arms apart and the pain from his dislocated shoulder nearly sends him to the edge of unconsciousness. The nails of his hands elongate and flash silver in the light.

A sharp odor of burnishing steel burns his nostrils and his metal nails warp before his eyes. Spreading, melding, stretching, they grow heavy and sharp. Darius screams—filling the air until he has no more and only a rasping whisper escapes his throat.

He stares horrified at the shining scythes attached to the meat of his hands. They slice through the air with a resonant sound, razor sharp, back and forth. The sweep his path takes is directly above the man's middle.

Nosferatu's bony claw rips the sackcloth off the head of the bound man.

He sees the whites of his eyes—his own eyes.

His face stares back at him, a mirror image. The inscription on the trophy tied to the man's hands reads plainly in etched letters: *Darius Pendleton.*

He is the pendulum, the mechanism of his demise. Darius

struggles against the metal scythe, seeking to slow the momentum and its bisecting purpose, but he only increases the speed of the blade and its descent.

What had been put in motion could not be stopped, it is of his own making.

Darius cries out at the inevitable slice of the pendulum through the man's wrists. The trophy splits in two and rolls to the one side of the man's body. Darius's throat sears in pain with a scream that produces no sound.

Blood streams from his own wrists and slides down the silver metal of the scythe, bisecting the dying man and ruined trophy. The roar from the monsters grows deafening and mingles with the terrible throbbing of his slit wrists.

Dark spots encroach his vision and all descends into blackness.

"Darius? Darius?" Jenna asks, hiding her amusement. "You're shaking."

The smart phone slips from Darius's tremulous fingers and he takes a step back. The glare of the fluorescent lights pierce his eyes and he stumbles backward, knocking two chairs over and hitting the floor hard. He scrambles to his feet, gropes at his wrists, examining them for the precise slice he'd inflicted only moments before but his inspections yield clean, intact skin and human fingernails.

Everyone in the room stares at him.

His gaze locks on Lucinda's, still dabbing at her coffee-soaked sweatshirt.

Darius points a shaky finger at her. "I know that one. 1961, *The Pit...*" he swallows hard, *"and the Pendulum."*

JASMINE ANGELL is an Arizona native living in Salt Lake City, Utah. On a daily basis she juggles the creative life with a happily energetic family life. In her free time she bakes extravagant cakes, crafts Steampunk costumes and eagerly plans her next mermaid tea party. Look for her YA fantasy novels at www.jasmineangell.com.

THE THIRD ATTEMPT

BY E. ELLIS ALLEN

His emasculation happened, not as a flood, but as a drip in a metal pan, building, building, building, until it crushed him. Had he been swayed to either love his wife more or to hate her less, they both may have come out unscathed.

Linus Beets Jr. was broken. Once considered the next great American Author, his debut novel, *Promises*, sold two million copies within the first year. Now he was nothing. His limelight dwindled and he had forgotten how to write. At first, he blamed luck, then perfection, and then his wife, Fancy.

He had felt the pangs of hunger for a while, though he didn't know what they meant. Linus wasn't hungry in the traditional sense—not starving—but something else altogether. It was a craving that turned and twisted his life looking for an escape. The hunger made him numb, in his hands, his mind, and his heart, so numb he even heard the buzz of nothingness in his ears.

He was certain, once satisfied, the pain would end, like a snake digesting its prey. The snake isn't hungry once it eats the rabbit. Until Linus knew what the hunger was exactly, he settled into a tedious life made up of menial tasks bookended by waking in the morning and going to bed at night, and this he blamed on Fancy.

Fancy Bernard-Wexler Beets was born better than Linus. She was raised in wealth and connection, and educated at the best schools. Fancy was exquisite, reinforced through years of hair appointments, manicures, gym memberships, and facials.

On a ski trip in Aspen, Fancy broke her tibia. Surgery followed in which a long metal rod was inserted in the front of her knee, down the bone marrow, and set with three screws, one at the top and two at the bottom, the thought of which turned his stomach. After, Linus became her nurse, her captive, her slave.

"Linus! My leg hurts!" Fancy whined. "Get in here, hurry!"

She was awake. She was awake and in pain, though not enough to silence her. Every three hours she wailed and ordered him to deaden her ache. Poor, delicate Fancy couldn't swallow her Percocet whole—even though it was gelatin coated.

"Help me, Linus."

So he did. No one told him it was dangerous to undo the painkiller capsule, although it may not have made a difference if they had. A wistful fog overcame Linus while he was in the kitchen pulling apart Fancy's pill. A tall, slender glass was filled with Diet Pepsi, and *Seinfeld* reruns blared from the television in the next room.

To escape both his reality and his spouse, Linus lost himself in a daydream. A gray haze wrapped around him like a cocoon. Mostly, he dreamed of how to murder Fancy—choking was a favorite, but a shove off a cliff worked, too. He imagined once or twice puncturing her body full of bullet holes but banished the idea because he was a pacifist and didn't own a gun.

In his dream, Linus climbed the stairs and entered her bedroom. Fancy was asleep. He opened her curtains exposing the full white moon. Moonlight absorbed into her skin shading it ghostly blue. The street was empty and dark, save for a few porch lights and lost traffic in the distance.

From his sleeve, Linus pulled a stretch of metal wire the width of fishing string. He moved to her bedside. He threaded the wire underneath her neck and wound it around twice before doing the same to each of his gloved hands. He pulled.

As the ligature tightened, Fancy's eyes fluttered open.

"How's this for not buying you jewelry? How 'bout a necklace?" he'd scream. "How's the fit, sweetheart? Comfortable?"

Her mouth gulped for air. He tightened the wire more. Her hands grasped at his. Her eyes went wide, pleading for him to stop. He continued to pull the cord, tighter, tighter, tighter, until her head popped off.... He'd always awoken before there was blood. Blood made him queasy.

In a trance, Linus dismantled a Percocet, and dropped the powdery contents into bubbling Diet Pepsi. He walked upstairs and handed the glass over. Fancy downed the drink. Linus left and went back to watching TV.

Around hour three, he checked on Fancy. The bell he'd given her at the hospital, a gag gift that backfired, hadn't rung for over an hour, maybe more. He opened the door of the master bedroom, her room now, not his. Her wounded leg was propped up on the pillows they once shared. Her cell phone lay next to her head and snores wedged her mouth open.

The next hour Linus returned. The snoring had stopped, and he studied her for the up and down motion of her breath moving in and out. It was hard to tell if it was.

He sensed rather than remembered what he had done. How

many pills had he put in Fancy's drink? One? Two? Seven? Eight? He didn't know.

Linus raced to the kitchen. He searched the garbage can. In the kitchen sink, elbow deep, he rooted around in the damp, dank disposal for medicine shells, without luck. The orange plastic prescription container was open on the counter. Linus counted the remaining pills. Two were missing.

Taking two stairs at a time, Linus sprinted back to check her pulse, it was faint and slow, but it was there. He tried rousing her, lifting her shoulders off the bed and shaking her. Nothing. He called her name and wiped her face with cold water. No response.

Horror settled on him while he sat at the top of the stairs; it penetrated his brain, spliced open the void and shined a light on the possibility of what he'd done. Linus had overdosed his wife.

What should he do? Was she dying? Should he call an ambulance? The police? Her doctor? Should he perform CPR? Did he know CPR?

From the bedroom, Fancy stirred and groaned. He dashed to her. Her eyes quivered open, and she smiled at him. He grabbed her hand.

"You're awake! I'm sorry! I accidentally gave you too many pills—"

"You've got to get out of here, Barry." Her words slipped and rolled around her tongue.

"No, Fancy, it's me, Linus." He held her hand; her palm rested on his chest, his heart.

"I'm serious, Barry. Linus will kill us if he finds us together."

Barry? Barry Wilcox, her personal trainer?

"Fancy?" Linus was unnerved but assumed it was her pills talking, not his wife. "It's me, Linus."

"Stop it, Barry!" Fancy's lip stuck out.

"Okay?" he said. She was confused and upset, rightfully so. After all, he had almost killed her. The least he could do was indulge her.

"Here, don't get upset. You're right. I'm Barry." As he spoke, a thread of thought wove its way to the front of his mind. "Remind me, are we sleeping together, Fancy?"

"Of course. You know that!" she giggled. "Remember last Tuesday? You ran out the back as Linus was pulling in the garage?"

He did remember a Tuesday, several Tuesdays ago, before the ski trip Fancy took with friends, when he had come up the driveway, parked the car, and entered the house. The back door was open, and their cat, Frisk, a chocolate Persian kitten, was gone. After arguing, Linus took the blame for not checking the door before he left the house that morning. He still hadn't found Frisk.

Linus's stomach dropped. The taste of pennies filled his mouth. The more he blinked, the more black dots swirled in front of him. He had to escape. He stumbled out of their old bedroom and down the hallway to his new room, the spare. The comfort of the gray haze coma he usually sought had evaporated.

Fancy and Barry Wilcox were having an affair? Barry— Barry rhymed with fairy. Wilcox—as in a willing cock, only plural—what a fitting name. Still, Barry? The stereotypical meathead, with his white toothy grin, waves of blonde hair, muscled arms and legs resembling braided bread. The Barry

Wilcox who didn't seem to own anything but tank tops and shorts?

Linus punched the wall, leaving an indent and cracked ivory paint in a circle. He didn't feel the weakness of pain; he felt the strength of hatred. He hated Fancy then, really and truly despised her. Had he a gun, he would have used it. Instead, he rifled through the small desk in the corner of the room, yanking out drawers and slamming them closed. Rage led him to an old legal pad, yellow and water stained in the bottom drawer, along with a blue pen. He took out the pair and climbed on his bed. He dwarfed the twin-sized bed, and his feet hung over the sides or off the end. Linus sat against the headboard and began to write; angrily, fervently, hungrily.

Early the next morning, before the sun cracked open the earth, Linus awoke with a jolt. The yellow notepad dropped from his cheek and flopped to the floor. Over forty pages of fiction covered the pad. For the first time in years, he had started a story, and as he transferred his words to his laptop, he noticed he didn't feel hungry.

————

WHEN BARRY WILCOX texted his well wishes to Fancy, this after two bouquets of daisies and then balloons, Linus used her phone and broke up with him. Barry protested. He said he would confront Linus, tell him Fancy didn't love him anymore, and ask for a divorce on her behalf. It was galling. Why would Fancy prefer a nobody to Linus Beets, Jr., the novelist?

Linus responded, posing as Fancy, and said she and Linus had reconciled. She asked Barry to leave her alone so she could make her marriage work. Still, Barry refused, which set in motion the second plan.

Because the breakup had been unexpected, Linus had already mixed two Xanax and Percocet and fed them to Fancy through a straw. He had no time to revive her before Barry came. Her unconscious, barely breathing state, however, could be used to his advantage.

At the top of the driveway, gripping the steering wheel, Linus waited. Fancy was passed out in the passenger seat. The house lights were off, as were the car headlights, but the engine was idling. He assumed Barry wouldn't park in front of the house, but down the hill. He expected that Barry would then jog —because everywhere the sex-sicle went he was jogging—up to the house.

Then, Linus would mow Barry down. He may have to roll over the man once or twice just to make sure. Linus would leave the car on top of him, move Fancy into the driver's seat and then go to bed.

Eventually, someone would notice the car flattening a dead man and Fancy passed out at the steering wheel. The neighbors would call the police, who would break the news to Linus as they dragged Fancy away in handcuffs. It was the perfect plan —two birds with one BMW.

Backlit by the streetlight, a figure emerged in the rearview mirror, walking up the drive with head bent over his phone. Linus threw the car in reverse. He sped down the driveway, tires screaming against the endless rows of square pavers. Linus's heart boomed in his chest as he careened towards his target.

Less than a foot away from taking Barry out, the car screeched to a halt. Linus had forgotten about a braking system that automatically activated and would not disengage. It wasn't fair.

"Linus? What's going on?" Barry asked in between gum chomps. He leaned inside the car and saw Fancy in the passenger seat.

"I'm taking Fancy to the emergency room," Linus lied. "Something's wrong with her." He hadn't anticipated Barry taking this as an invitation to join them.

As the two men sat in the waiting room at Amberhurst Hospital, Fancy had her stomach pumped, and Barry broke down. He confessed to the affair and then blamed himself for her apparent attempted suicide.

"She tried to break it off with me," Barry bawled. "But I wouldn't let her."

Barry said he was sorry and promised to leave Linus and Fancy alone. Linus shook the man's hand and forgave him. He even gave the idiot cab fare. So it wasn't exactly two birds, but one, and Linus took it.

THE YELLOW PAGE in front of Linus lay dormant and he couldn't get his pen to write. He struggled to track the path the story was going, only to find himself lost in the fiction-telling woods with both his hands and his mind frozen.

From his back pocket, his cell phone buzzed. Penelope Port, his agent, was calling. Before she could fire him, Linus told her about his newest idea and that he'd written one hundred pages so far—a lie, it had only been fifty-six—and he would send her the first forty. She was thrilled.

Down the hallway came the sound of a ringing bell. Fancy

rang and rang and rang until it deflated any creative thought in his head. Linus straightened and plastered a smile on his face.

"What's the matter, sweetheart?" he asked, entering her bedroom. Fancy turned and glared at him.

"When did you start calling me sweetheart?"

"Does it matter? What's wrong?"

"It's Barry. We were supposed to meet for physical therapy today but when I texted to confirm he told me he wasn't my trainer anymore. He said he'd given me to someone else."

"What?" Linus pretended to care.

"It must've been those painkillers! I must've texted him last week, and made him mad, but I can't find those messages."

She sank against the pillows lining the headboard, and her bottom lip stuck out. Fancy barely remembered having her stomach pumped, which led to the quick removal of all Percocet pills and no more refills per Doctor Nelson's orders.

"I'm sorry, sweetheart," Linus said. "I deleted those messages."

"Why?"

"They would've traumatized you again." He inched next to Fancy and stroked her hair. "We shouldn't talk about this right now. We just adjusted your medication—"

"I'm not going to kill myself," she said. Her voice was steady. "Tell me."

"Fine. You must've gotten the two of us mixed up because you sent Barry your suicide note. You said you loved me, but couldn't keep living a lie."

Fancy's eyes widened. He could see all the way around each of her irises. Her breath caught in her chest. It was delicious.

"I'm sorry, this is too much. I shouldn't have reminded you. Do you still want me to move back in here?"

"Move back? You mean in this room?"

"I know. I wasn't ready to reconcile before, but I am now if you still want me."

"Reconcile?"

"Wait, that is the lie you were talking about, right? The fact that we weren't living as husband and wife anymore?"

She stared at the wall in front of her. Her color drained past her neck, and her lips parted. Fancy turned, considered Linus, then nodded slightly.

"So it's settled?" Linus asked.

"Uh huh."

"Good!" Linus hurried around the bed and scooped her up as if carrying his bride across the threshold. He kissed her forehead and moved her to the bathroom to begin the process of cleaning and redressing her wounds.

Fancy smiled at Linus; it was small and almost indiscernible, but it was genuine, and it was for him. Perhaps their marriage was salvageable after all.

LIFE HAD RESUMED to what it was before the Aspen trip, but not to the way it was when they were first married. The two shared a room and a bed, but Linus rarely slept there. Instead, he retreated to his spare room, to his notepads and writing.

The excitement of the first pages he'd written had abandoned him and refused to return. He was blocked, angry, and hungry once again.

A light tap sounded on his door. Fancy was mobile with crutches, and as long as she didn't try using them down the steep staircase by herself, she could go anywhere. She had also weaned herself off all her antidepressants and Xanax, which only infuriated Linus.

Now she was awake and bored. Without Barry Wilcox, she was also lonely and annoying. Linus had thought about reuniting the two, but it left a bitter taste in his mouth.

Linus winced at Fancy's manicured fingernails rapping at his door. He hoped one would break off. Painfully.

"What?" he snapped.

"Can I come in?"

"No."

"Come on, Linus, unlock the door."

Linus rubbed circles into his forehead. He huffed to the door and opened it wide enough for one eye.

"Hello?" Fancy asked.

"I'm working."

"Can I read any of it yet?"

"No."

"Well, I thought we could go out to dinner tonight. I'm dying to get dressed up and be anywhere but here. Aren't you?" She moved within inches of Linus's eye.

"Can't. Working."

"Come on Linus, let me in!" She shoved against the door, knocking a red crease into Linus's forehead and cheek. He staggered back, holding his face.

"Sorry!" She laughed. "I forgot how close you were standing!"

He didn't believe her. She knew what she was doing. Fancy ignored Linus and hobbled past him to his workstation. She leaned her crutches against his desk. She maneuvered the lamplight above the yellow notepad and skimmed over the words.

"Remember," he said, biting his thumbnail, "It's just the first draft."

She nodded, lifting the pad and reading. She flipped to the next page and then read several more pages after that. Something flashed across her face. What it was, he didn't know. She flattened the sheets and placed them on the desktop.

"Well?" he asked. "What do you think?"

"Umm, what happens next?" she asked, "Does he kill his wife or does she catch on and call the police?"

Linus studied Fancy for a long stretch without answering. Did she suspect it was autobiographical? How far into the story had she read? She fidgeted.

"It's a dark comedy, right?" she asked, staring past him at the door. "An author who only gets inspired when he tries to kill his wife? It's clever." Her throat had gone dry, which was evident from the way she tried swallowing again and again.

He brightened. "Yes. Does it work? Is it funny enough?"

"Sure," she said. Her giggle was nervous. He moved around her and wrapped his arms about her waist. She stiffened. He rested his head on her shoulder. Her pulse hurled against the skin in her neck.

"I mean, it's no *Promises*," her voice caught. "What does Penelope think?"

"She agrees with you. She says it's still too rough, but thinks it's going somewhere. She wants me to go darker with it, though."

"Darker?"

"Yeah, but, how much darker can I go?" he asked. "Have any ideas?"

He could see the vein in her neck raised and pulsing even out of his peripheral. He spun her around.

"What's the matter, sweetheart?" he asked. "Your heart's really pumping. You're sweating. You're not having Percocet withdrawals, are you?"

Fancy's hand flew to her chest. She stepped back, but the desk was in her way. The dim light of the lamp was bisected by the lampshade, throwing circular light directly up to the ceiling and down on the desk.

"I'm fine," she said.

"No you're not," he touched her face. "I guess I've been neglecting you. It's all this stress and worry about writing another bestseller. Sorry, I upset you. Now that you mention it, I am hungry."

Linus kissed the bottom side of her wrist then handed her the crutches. He flipped on the bedroom light and caught a look of relief settle on Fancy's face.

"I guess I can stop working for the night."

"Great! I thought you could wear that burgundy jacket of yours with a blue tie?"

"I hate that jacket," he said. "Besides, I'd prefer ordering in."

"But I just said I wanted to eat out." Fancy's eyes narrowed, shooting flaming arrows at him. "Linus, I need to get out of this stinking house! I'm suffocating here." She looked him up and down. "And you look a mess."

He said nothing.

"The burgundy jacket will make you look presentable in public."

Linus watched her amble out of the room and down the hall. A gray cloud fell around her and he was dreaming once again. He could see her silhouette inside the haze. She was limping— weak—an easy kill.

He fantasized about her toppling down the staircase—head, feet, head, feet—and it fueled his appetite. The sound of her head cracking against the wall and stairs sent butterflies into his stomach. Skull fragments piercing her brain made Linus feel warm and fuzzy all the way down to his toes.

When awareness brought him back, Fancy had passed the stairs and was already in her bedroom. He heard the shuffle, slide, shuffle of her leg boot against the Italian marble on the bathroom floor. She was heading to the closet, hunting for his ugly jacket. Once found, along with some horrible blue tie, she'd parade him around like a dog on a pinstriped leash. He wouldn't let that happen. He got an idea.

"Linus?" she called. "You coming?"

"Give me five minutes."

Linus quickly outlined the story's ending. He placed his notepad in the bottom desk drawer and left his room.

The length of the hall shifted, growing long and winding. He turned off the switch that operated the lamp on the hall table and unscrewed the light bulb. A light in the kitchen was on. The television was off.

Skipping the squeaking top step, Linus crept downstairs. He flicked off the kitchen light and turned on the TV and upped it to almost full volume to suppress any other noise a neighbor might hear. A blue strobe bounced off the ceiling, the couches, and the floor. It flashed across the kitchen and made it's way to the handrail, illuminating it. Linus opened the junk drawer and found a Phillips screwdriver.

He sidled along the staircase and loosened the screws securing the handrail to the wall. Linus rushed up the rest of the flight and unscrewed the railing's top fasteners, before stopping to collect his breath.

Once inside the master bedroom, Linus turned out the light. He placed the screwdriver on his dresser. Fancy's cell phone rested on the bed. It buzzed. He turned off her phone and pocketed it before heading to the bathroom.

The glare of the closet's light filtered across the bathroom tile. Fancy was in there. The sound of metal hangers sliding back and forth was louder than the sitcom laugh track booming downstairs.

He slipped off his shoes and placed them behind the door. Fancy's crutches leaned on the other side, against the door jam. He sneaked them to the bottom of the tub. He listened at the door. She was talking to herself in a barrage of frustration over her clothes and the boot she wore on her leg. Linus moved, and the floor groaned underneath him.

"Linus?"

He closed his eyes. It would be over soon. He opened his eyes and inhaled. Now, to pick a fight with his wife. He walked in to find her half dressed. She wore a white button-down shirt and was attempting to pull on a pair of trousers. A pant leg was lying in a puddle around her booted foot.

"How 'bout a skirt?" he asked.

"You're giving me fashion advice?" He saw her try to smile at him, but it waned and flattened on her lips. "That's not the kind of help I need from you."

Fancy pointed to her boot and held onto the clothes rod. Linus rolled down her slacks. Small black hairs stippled her leg, making it rough and prickled. He let his fingers drag up and down them.

"What? You think you don't have to shave your legs for me anymore?"

"You're one to talk!" Fancy retorted. "You look like a mountain man or an Alaskan logger."

"Right. Want to play that game? Let's play!"

He yanked the pant leg off the toe of her boot. She howled. Linus snatched a handful of dresses and threw them to the floor.

"These make you look like your mother," he said.

"Stop it!"

He ignored her and ransacked the other side of the closet, pulling sweaters and pants she had given him over the years. He threw them in a pile.

"What are you doing?"

"Making kindling," he said. "I mean everything I own looks like crap, right? We can't possibly go out with me looking like this. Maybe I should just stick to tank tops and shorts like your good pal Barry?"

"What are you talking about? What about Barry?"

"He was there, while you got your stomach pumped," Linus said. He flashed her a fake smile. "He told me everything. Still, I forgave you."

"Oh, Linus."

Linus spun around and headed in the direction of the bedroom. She snagged his arm. He shrugged out of her grasp.

"Let's talk about this—" Fancy called after him.

"No. I'm starving. We're eating in. Sushi for two, sound good?" He called over his shoulder. He hadn't forgotten Fancy was allergic to fish.

Fancy's anxiety sparked shocks inside him that warmed his blood. Linus hurried down the hall to his room. He could faintly hear Fancy walk through the bathroom. She'd look for her crutches and then her cell phone. Linus tapped the rectangle he'd shoved into his pocket earlier. He waited, his eyes adjusting to the dark.

Fancy was in the hall. The light switch in the hallway clicked twice, but the lamp never went on.

"Linus?" she called. She probably assumed he was sulking on the couch, watching *Seinfeld*. He grinned. It was working. The whole plan was falling into place. His pulse quickened, and saliva filled his mouth. This was it! He was the snake and Fancy was the rabbit.

From the door of the spare bedroom, Linus tracked her. He squinted. Fancy's pace was glacial without her crutches.

A squeak from the floor alerted Linus that she was descending the staircase. He slithered into position against the adjacent wall. She held onto the railing with each hand, lumbering down a step at a time.

He peered around the corner. The flares of light from the television made Fancy's movements shudder like a stop motion film. She was on the fourth step. He pounced.

The top stair squeaked under Linus's weight. Her head snapped to the side.

"Linus?"

He lunged at her. He pushed, knocking her off balance. She tipped and threw her limbs around the railing. Something glinted from her right hand. The rail shook free from the wall and collapsed in Fancy's arms. Her head bent down and she dropped the bar.

Linus sped towards her, his hands poised to shove her one last time. She spun around and screamed.

He didn't realize what had punctured his side until he saw the yellow handle of the screwdriver protruding out of him. He felt no pain as he pitched forward, down the staircase, headfirst.

He felt no anger either. He was falling, not into a gray fog but into nothingness.

———

IT WAS the beeps and gasps of machines that awakened Linus, followed by a stench of antiseptic. He opened his eyes. The burn of florescent light blurred objects into one before separating them. He was in a hospital room. Something fat was propped in his mouth and he couldn't move his neck. At first, he assumed he was tied down, but he couldn't wiggle his fingers or his toes.

Fancy leaned over a plant, watering it with a plastic cup. A large silver Mylar balloon sticking out of the pot said, "Get Well Soon."

"Sweetheart, you're awake again," she cooed. "The doctor called and said you were conscious." She sat down on his hospital bed and crossed her once broken leg. A red scar ran down the front of her shiny and newly shaven shin.

"Let me catch you up. You had a bad spill in the house and didn't land well. We must have been a sight when the police came—you, broken at the bottom of the stairs and me, wearing a just a blouse and panties. I told the cops you were fixing the handrail, making it more secure so I wouldn't fall, when you slipped and fell on the screwdriver. It's so… so… what's the word? Ironic! They agreed it was all a crazy accident." Fancy laughed. "Do you know what paraplegic means? Don't worry, you will."

Linus blinked, searching for the soft gray haze of a dream.

"I got a hold of Penelope Port," Fancy went on. "We're going ahead with your book. Of course, I'll fill in the ending with your final notes. You know, I never understood your hunger to write before; there is something to it. Also, your treatment is going to be slow and painful. But Barry has agreed to help with your physical therapy. We've been talking and meeting a lot…"

Though she kept talking, Fancy went soundless. For a moment, panic seized him, encasing him in a blood red cloud. It was then that Linus realized his big mistake. In all the time he spent quenching his hunger—of being the snake—he'd never considered what it was like for the rabbit.

Linus couldn't move. He couldn't fight. The familiar hum of nothingness filled his ears, whispering. It was hungry, too. Numbness sprang on him, coiled around him, and devoured him from the head down. The only power left for him was to concede.

E. ELLIS ALLEN is schizophrenic when it comes to writing; she writes Fiction and Nonfiction, gravitates towards Short Story Horror, thinks in Science Fiction, and her hobbies include writing Essays for her blog. She currently lives in South Jordan, Utah with her husband, two kids, and her crazy pet Chiweenie.

GHOSTED

BY TERRI BARANOWSKI

He didn't have to die. That's the thing that haunts me still, even after all this time. My sweet husband was intelligent, witty, handsome. Loyal. We were only twenty-eight years old when he chose to end his life. An arranged gun, a loaded decision, and the love of my life was gone, off to whatever awaited him in the eternities.

Twelve years is a long time to live alone, a long time to sleep in an empty bed, but I have my faith to get me through. Only the power of God could help a woman in her thirties live a life of celibacy, especially when that woman has a slutty sister like Resha. Just last night she talked me into going clubbing.

"You need a girl's night out, Anna," she'd said. "Just a little dancing."

But when a cute guy asked me to dance, she whispered in my ear, "You can have the keys to my truck if you wanna, uhm, you know, have a little fun."

I didn't even know the man's name. What kind of a girl does she think I am?

Now here she is in my kitchen, wearing my favorite hoodie, drinking coffee, and nagging about my social life, as if I need another reminder that I'm almost 40, childless, and single.

"I'm just sayin', Anna," Resha said, "it's not healthy for a woman to ignore her sexuality and live like a... a... robot. If there's a God, I'm sure He gets that."

"It's not about God's understanding. I made an agreement."

"I know, I know, covenants and priestesses and forever relationships. You've told me a jillion times but I saw the way you looked at that dude in the produce department the other day. You're hungry. If I hadn't hollered, 'Pineapple' I think you'd have done him right there."

"Yeah, I meant to ask you about that."

"What, how to go about it? I know it's been twelve years but, geez, you haven't forgotten, have you?"

"Of course not. Don't be ridiculous. Why's everything always about sex with you?"

"Because it is. What did you want to ask me?"

She seemed annoyed but I went ahead anyway.

"What on earth is that pineapple thing about? Does it have anything to do with that sponge character?"

"Never mind." Resha rolled her eyes.

"I'm serious."

"So am I. You're my baby sister and I'm worried about you." She looked sincere. "You need to get out more, Anna. Meet people. You're spending too much time alone and starting to act a little weird, all culty."

"I told you, I'm working on a book and just because I'm not ashamed to talk about our father in heaven doesn't make me a fanatic," I said.

"What about online dating? I heard there's a new app where

women call the shots, make the connections, and plan the first meet-ups. I think it's called Mari Me."

I laughed so hard I nearly choked on my chai tea.

"I know, hilarious, right? But it's spelled M-a-r-i. She's supposed to be a goddess who controls the weather or something. I think it's kinda clever."

"Women run the show?" I was intrigued.

"Yeah, cool, right? No more dozens and dozens of creepy "Hey, cutie" messages from sleazy dudes who just want to score without putting forth the effort."

"Uhm, yeah, I don't think I'd have that problem anyway. I'm a boring book nerd, into mythology and religion. I've never really fit in, at least not here in Summer, Utah. Guys are looking for girls like you, Resha. Blonde hair, blue-eyed, toned, flirty, a girly-girl who knows how to feed a man's ego. Summer Barbies. Not demure girls with dark hair, dark eyes, and cappuccino-colored skin."

"Don't be ridiculous, Anna. You're a goddess. Men would *die* for you. Besides, the beauty of this app is that we don't have to worry about what they want. It's all about what we want— who, what, when, where, and how. We decide."

Either Resha had perfected her powers of persuasion or my twelve-year drought was weakening my resolve.

"I'll think about it," I said.

———

I GUESS "I'll think about it" translated to "let's do it!" in Resha's mind because the very next day she called to break the news that she'd created a Mari Me account in my name.

"Don't worry," she said, "I signed up, too. We can try it

together. It'll be an adventure." My sister, the unsolicited travel agent. She'd be the first to book me a one-way ticket to Hades if she could.

"What do I have to do?" I asked.

"Download the app. I texted you your user name and password."

I hurried off the phone to see what new chaos Resha had created in my life. The pics she posted were from our Cancun vacation. They made me seem a lot more outgoing and were surprisingly flattering. What harm could come from browsing through profiles? I clicked on the tab marked "Mr. Right."

What kind of self-respecting guy joins a dating app? I texted Resha.

Have you found the Mr. Right tab? she replied, ignoring my bad attitude. *Be sure to use the filters.*

But she was too late. I was already swiping right. Again and again.

Oooo, look at that stud!

And again.

That night, I cuddled into bed with my phone to check the responses to my likes, not at all sure what to expect. I wasn't very popular in high school and only had a couple of boyfriends in college, why would I get a lot of interest now that I'm almost forty?

To my extraordinary delight and absolute amazement, every guy responded positively. Now it was up to me to initiate a conversation. But I needed more time. Later, I was browsing Facebook when I received a message from Enzo, a guy I'd partnered with on a college writing project. We had a few mutual friends and he'd noticed a humorous comment I'd made on one of their posts.

Anna, that's hilarious. It's good to find you. You look fabulous! Married life must be treating you well.

So I had to explain the awful facts about my late husband.

Enzo had also lost a spouse, only his loss was on account of his wife running off with their fertility doctor. Fertility issues, another thing we had in common. Our conversation went from catch-up to profundities to playfulness, and cycled back around, with Enzo occasionally commenting on the serendipitousness of our social media meet up. I may have considered the possibility had he not moved to London. In any case, it was fun to practice flirting, even if through texts. At some point, I mentioned the twelve-year thing and he responded with a barrage of exclamation points. !!!!!!!!!!!! Probably twelve. Not that I counted. We chatted for several hours that night, and the next, and the night after that, when I told him about my foray into online dating and the men from Mari Me. His response caught me off guard.

Wouldn't you rather be with an old friend than a complete stranger?

Hm, great question, was my ingenious response, but I added the thinking emoji for effect.

Enzo had a proposition.

I'm flying into Salt Lake next week to meet with a client. Can I take you to dinner? How about Martine's? I've been dying to try their semolina-crusted trout filet.

They don't have semolina-crusted trout filet in London? I almost replied, but then realized his appetite had nothing to do with food.

———

I DECIDED to pick Enzo up at his hotel. If I drove, I could maintain some semblance of control. It was April and spring was blooming all over the valley. I wondered if I looked too eager… too desperate… too twelve-year abstinence-ish. You can't go wrong with a classic, little black dress, I thought. Hair in a chignon, tiny pearl earrings, light makeup, and the shiny black Christian Louboutin's with the five-inch red and black stiletto heel and red leather outsole that I found for a steal at a posh secondhand boutique in Park City. Had I overdone it?

As I nervously waited in the lobby, I prayed for guidance. Dewey never really liked Enzo. I was having second thoughts when the elevator doors opened. The huge grin on Enzo's face and the look in his eyes as they scanned me from head to toe told me that he was pleased. I wished I could say the same. Who wears a flannel shirt to a dinner date? Or ridiculous sneakers. And he hadn't even bothered to shave. I had trouble masking my disappointment. Fortunately, the dinner conversation and delectable food made up for Enzo's underwhelming appearance.

We talked effortlessly about everything from business to music and then the sexy elephant in the room had to be acknowledged.

"So… how did you ever make it twelve years without…?" Enzo proceeded with caution. His hesitance was ever so disarming.

"I was determined and committed," I explained.

"Was?" He raised his eyebrows and appeared to be trying to restrain himself from jumping up and down with glee.

"Yeah, those Mari Me guys aren't really looking for eternal companions and I don't plan on marrying again anyway, so why not? Twelve years seems to have been sufficient time to…" I shut my mouth before I said too much.

"Well, then, may I suggest that ending the fast with a friend who cares about you is a better alternative to those Mari Me schmoes you were pursuing?"

"I was not pursuing," I said. "I was merely browsing."

Enzo laughed and switched to a safer subject, our favorite professor, who taught Shakespeare.

"Remember when he took two weeks off to go to India? What the heck was that about?"

"That was weird," I said. "He came back so enthralled with the culture that we watched Bollywood movies for the rest of the semester."

"Do you remember their rendition of *Othello?* It was intense. What was it called?"

"*Omcara*. I have it on DVD. It's one of my favorites."

So of course we went to my place to watch the tragedy.

I was preparing Enzo's drink in the kitchen when he quietly came up behind me, put his arms around my waist, and started tenderly kissing my neck. I could feel myself slipping. It had been so long.

"Tell me if you want me to stop," he whispered.

I wasn't at all sure about this but then Enzo slowly began unzipping my little black dress and I was undone.

———

ENZO HAD BEEN a quick and selfish lover and I was glad to see him go. If that's what I'd been missing then it really hadn't been a sacrifice at all. I decided to give Mari Me another try. There had to be someone looking for more than just a night of hanging at the Y. Someone of substance.

Swipe right for Gene, a debonair-looking geologist. Gene was in his early fifties and claimed to be looking for a long-term relationship. He'd only been married once. The travel demands of his career had taken their toll, resulting in an amicable parting of ways. He loved his life but was lonely and looking for companionship. We met for lunch. He was attentive, well mannered, and knew how to treat a lady. I invited him to the opera for our next date. Puccini's *Turandot*. He was a good sport and dressed to kill so of course I invited him back to my place. Twelve years had proven a sufficient sacrifice. I knew that Dewey approved. Besides, after the bad experience with Enzo, I was curious.

Spending the night with Gene had turned out to be the perfect antidote for the awfulness that was Enzo. Gene may have been much older but he was strong and patient and eager to please. Afterward, we cuddled in bed and shared our favorite songs and the stories behind them. Gene wasn't afraid to be open and vulnerable. I wondered if this could be the one. If not, I wouldn't regret this night. Surely it couldn't be wrong to connect with another human being on an emotional, intellectual, and physical level. Comforting each other. It seemed as if spending the night alone, in our separate beds, would have been the greater sin. As if reading my mind, he pulled me closer and we fell asleep in each other's arms.

In the morning, Gene thanked me, handed me a pile of cash "for the opera tickets, gas, and whatever" and told me he'd be in touch but was leaving tomorrow for a huge project in New Zealand and wouldn't be back for a few years. I was stunned and insulted but said, "Can you stay for one last drink? A goodbye toast?"

"Of course," he said.

———

OK, I get it now. No matter what I post on my profile, no matter what the dude claims, it all comes down to one thing. At first I thought my sister's fun-loving portrayal of me was attracting the wrong crowd—guys who thought fun equaled one-night-stand. So I made things clear—*looking for a long-term commitment, not interested in a hook up*. I thought that was more likely to appeal to the kind of guy I needed—a man who cared about family and eternity. But dudes just thought that meant they'd have to work a little harder to get some. Even guys who professed to be religious or claimed they were looking for an eternal companion, guys who listed "monogamous" as their relationship preference. Age, education, income—none of it mattered. They all wanted the same thing. Every last right-swiping one of them.

What the hell, I may as well cut right to the chase. Why waste time? Who needs the self-esteem annihilating disappointment? I searched profiles for the hottest hunk I could find. Swipe right, Silas. Twenty-eight—same age as you, my love. Dark, wavy hair. Eyes to get lost in. Lips. Dear God, those lips. And speaking of God, to say he had the body of a Greek god would be a lie. No Greek god ever looked *that* good. I could grab onto those muscular arms and stare at that six-pack until I OD'd on dopamine.

Silas.

My heart races even now.

Bless his soul, he tried to be a gentleman and arrange a proper date but I wasn't having it. Why bother? No, baby, let's just go for a ride and "talk." (I caught on to their lingo real quick.) So I picked him up and we drove around for maybe, uhm, ten minutes, then I told him I knew a great spot at Utah Lake. He smiled. Geez, that guy was adorable.

I parked in a dark and secluded area. Moonlight reflecting on water lit our way. We got out and kissed. Unbelievably, he was the most passionate kisser ever. You'd think with a body like that, he wouldn't try so hard, but no.

"I like your skirt," he whispered, as his hand started to explore.

It was out of this world incredible, perfect in every way. The mood, the setting, his body, his skilled execution. Perfection.

I wanted Silas, needed Silas, more than air. Every quark within came alive and hungered for all of him. We got a little rowdy up against my car. And a little rowdier. Then a whole heck of a lot rowdier. A low-flying helicopter approached. Oddly out of place, it should have halted our passion, or at least slowed it down. Instead, it had the opposite effect. The chopper reached us and was flying directly overhead at the exact… right… moment.

I'm still not sure what that was all about. Search and rescue?

But the night wasn't over. There was much more fun to be had. In the front seat of my Highlander. On the back seat. In the far back, twice. Who knew having a roof inches above your head could be so advantageous? Then we climbed up on the hood, lay back, and watched the stars. And had more fun. I couldn't get enough of Silas. You'd think it would be exhausting but, on the contrary, it was energizing. Fortunately, I brought a bottle of wine to help us relax. It was the greatest night of my life. And that was the end of Silas.

I still miss him.

———

"Ghosting," Resha said as we had lunch at a sidewalk café. It was mid-July and way too hot to be eating outdoors, yet there we were.

"Isn't that my dress you're wearing?" I said, annoyed.

"Don't change the subject, Anna."

"No, I really wanna know."

"You know it is."

"Well, how'd you get it? I don't remember giving it to you."

"You know I have a key."

"That doesn't mean you have the right to go into my house and help yourself to my things, Resha." I was pretty pissed. "When are you going to start acting like the goddess that you are?"

"Huh?"

"Never mind."

"Alright, I'm sorry. I had a date with Max. Do you want me to take it off right now? I will but I still think you're deflecting."

"It's fine. Just please ask next time," I said, knowing she wouldn't. "And who's Max?"

"Remember the accountant that I met on Mari Me? The one with four kids and a vacation home in Oregon?"

"Uhm, I think so. Is he the one you went camping with?"

"Yep. Today is our two-month anniversary. I think he might be the one, Anna. Just the other day he told me he's in love with me."

"I'm happy for you, Resh. Just… be careful.

"I know, I know, happy endings are just for fairy tales. I get it. But maybe…"

"So what about ghosts?" I interrupted that nonsense.

"Ghost*ing*. It's when someone you're dating suddenly ceases all communication with you because they're too chicken-shit to tell you that they aren't interested anymore. That's what these pussies have been doing to you. Ghosting."

"Hm," was all I could muster. What else could I say?

———

I SHOULD HAVE KNOWN BETTER. Something was not quite right with Jeremy from the beginning. For one thing, he wanted to correspond on some obscure messaging app and his texts were often off-the-wall or contentious. Still, I was enjoying the banter and he could be so clever and engaging that, when he asked to meet, I agreed.

I picked him up at his friend's house and he asked me to come in and meet Hiram. I really didn't want to but he insisted. Hiram's house made me uncomfortable. Empty cans of cat food and pizza boxes were strewn across the floor and dirty plates and silverware covered the table. A peculiar odor permeated the air and I had to breathe through my mouth to keep from retching.

Jeremy introduced me as if I were the first girl he'd ever dated and he was proud to show me off. After introductions, they left me standing in the kitchen and went in the living room, where I could see Jeremy hand Hiram an envelope. Hiram carefully opened it and removed a wad of cash, which he counted. Nodding, he slapped Jeremy on the back. "Good job," he said, "maybe you're not such a misfit, after all."

"Nice meeting you," I hollered from the kitchen, and hastily made my way for the door. Jeremy followed.

"I know he's a little weird," Jeremy whispered, "but we've been friends since grade school."

I didn't respond. We drove to an archery range and spent the next few hours competing and comparing techniques then had dinner at some hole-in-the-wall barbecue joint widely noted for its ribs, which really weren't all that great. I asked our server for to-go cups of Coke.

In the car, I took a flask from the glove compartment and poured into Jeremy's cup.

"Need a little pick-me-up after that butt-kicking I gave you on the range?" I asked.

"For sure but what about you? You could use a little something to calm you down a bit."

"Yeah, but I'm driving."

"Your loss. Whaddya wanna do now?"

Bored, I considered the options. Best as I could tell, it was down to two: either we were going to have sex or I was going to go home and do some writing. But my book, *Tablets of Destiny,* the book that would be my legacy, wasn't calling out to me.

"Your house?" I asked.

"No can do," Jeremy said matter-of-factly, without explanation.

After learning that my sister was prone to dropping by unannounced, my house was out of the question.

"We can find a nice bed and breakfast near Park City. There are great deals this time of year," I said.

"Nah, let's just do that Holiday Inn right there." He pointed.

As luck would have it, we were stopped at a red light directly in front of the hotel.

———

"Room 412." Jeremy laughed as he opened the door. "According to HTTP, this is a bad idea."

"What? Why?"

"Oh, it's just programming talk for something that's unworkable."

"We didn't need code to tell us that, did we?"

Jeremy snorted.

"Do you want to text your family and let them know where you are?" he said.

"Uhm… should I?"

But Jeremy didn't respond. He was sitting at the edge of the bed, busily unpacking a backpack. The weirdness was unsettling.

Vial of essential oil.

Foreplay?

Jeremy opened the vial and began dabbing all over his body.

What the hell?

Duct tape.

"Oh hey, I'm totally not into that," I said.

"What? Oh no, this is just stuff for when Hiram and I go camping."

What the fuck?

A rubber mask, of the creepy variety.

Ok, I'm out.

But I was too terrified to talk. This is what I get for playing a dangerous game. It's time to pay the piper.

"Come sit down." Jeremy patted the bed next to him.

And just like a horror movie trope, I did.

To my relief and then astonishment, he quickly put all of the paraphernalia away and began taking off his clothes. Never had I been so confused. Maybe he was just socially awkward.

Stripped down to his boxers, Jeremy hopped up on the bed and began massaging my neck and shoulders.

"Are you okay?" he asked. "You seem tense."

"Just a little nervous. It's been awhile," I lied.

"Calm down, just relax, it'll be okay," my killer said as he kissed my head.

I whispered a silent prayer but felt abandoned. All I could think to do was play along, bide time, so I let him have his way with me. He was clumsy and awkward, as if this were his first time. I'd hoped he'd wear himself out and fall asleep so I could escape but he just kept getting more hyper.

Suddenly, he jumped up and started howling. Climbing up on the windowsill, arms splayed, he pressed his naked body against the glass.

"Get down from there, Jeremy. Someone's going to call the police."

But Jeremy either didn't hear or care. He continued to howl and move his body against the glass. I slowly got out of bed and started dressing. This got his attention and he jumped from windowsill to bed to floor in rapid succession.

"Where ya goin', babe? Huh? Huh? HUH?" He was talking fast and loud and looking wild, out of control.

I wondered if he were on something, but then remembered the flask.

"Jeremy, hon, I'm cold. Come here. Lie back down and keep me warm."

He hesitated, as if considering his next move.

My cell phone rang opportunistically. I cautiously moved to the nightstand, one eye on Jeremy. He sat down as I picked up the phone. Resha's face appeared on the screen

"Sorry, I have to get this, it's my sister," I explained.

Jeremy nodded.

"Anuh… whereareyou... Ineedyou… Max… broke up with me." Resha was crying and barely comprehensible.

"I'm in Room 412 at the Holiday Inn with Jeremy, the guy I met on Mari Me who likes archery, remember I told you?"

I gave as much info as possible in case I ended up missing.

"Oh, I'm... I'm... sorry." Resha sniffed.

"I'll be right there, love. Your house?" I asked, fully embracing the opportunity.

"No, your house."

"I'm on the way, Resh," I said as I made my way toward the door, but Jeremy was up and rushing after me.

"I'll wait here for you but can you leave that flask?" he asked.

So I did.

———

I HURRIED HOME, my mind racing. Everything felt surreal and I couldn't shake a terrifying sense of foreboding. I drove faster. Peeling into my driveway, I slammed the brakes, threw the car in park, and rushed to get inside. Opening the door, I called Resha's name.

"In the bedroom," she called.

As soon I entered my room, I realized that I'd been played. Resha stood next to my desk, a look of horror on her tearstained face. *Tablets of Destiny* blazed from my laptop screen. I couldn't believe I had forgotten to shut it down. I was usually pretty careful. No one was supposed to see it. My book... Holy Scripture... my legacy. They wouldn't understand. I grabbed the laptop, closed the file, and logged off.

"I can explain, Resha." I tried, but she wasn't having it.

"You think you're Inanna? The goddess of… of…"

"Earth, love, fertility, and war," I said, "and I don't think it. I *know* it."

Resha looked as if she'd been hoping I'd deny it.

"If you think about it, Sis, it all makes sense. You and I, total opposites. Inanna and Ereshkigal."

"You killed Dewey! I thought you loved him."

"No, Resha. I still love him. He's my one and only eternal companion."

"You're a murderer! How could you?" She was crying, screaming, shaking her head.

"Please listen to me," I said.

She nodded but kept crying.

I said, "I'd always had the feeling that I didn't belong here, that there was more to my life. I prayed and prayed and one day, when I was about sixteen, the God of Wisdom, our Father, Enki, appeared to me and revealed my true identity and destiny. It was such a comfort.

"Imagine my surprise when Dewey and I were unable to have children. We tried everything yet nothing worked. Me, the goddess of fertility. It really shook my faith. I was worried I'd imagined it, that I was crazy or it was all a lie. I was so depressed, so dejected. I fasted and prayed but it was like talking to the ceiling. I had to know. There was no other way. I had to end my life on earth so I could ask Enki why."

"But you're still here." Resha said.

"I had it all planned. Dewey was at work. The gun was loaded and I was writing a goodbye note. For some reason, he came home for lunch and caught me. As soon as he walked in, I grabbed the gun so he couldn't stop me but he begged and pleaded. I said I was sorry but I had to. I told him to stay here because he deserved to find a Summer Barbie to have a family with."

It was hard to talk about what happened next.

"He got down on his knees, crying, said he felt helpless to satisfy my hunger to bear children, to provide the most precious and important gift, that it was all his fault, he was powerless, and the only way he could regain power was if I'd let him take my place. He'd find Enki and learn what we needed to do, and then prepare a place for us in the eternities, where we could have children forever and ever. I didn't want to let him do it but I couldn't bear to see him so unhappy."

"So you shot him?"

"We pulled the trigger together."

"But what happened to those other men? Are they dead?"

"It's all here, in the Scriptures I've been called to write." I motioned toward the laptop. "I couldn't bear to live without Dewey. He didn't come back to tell me what to do. I vowed to remain celibate until I got an answer. While browsing the profiles of those guys, Dewey's spirit finally came to me. He'd help me choose the men and I'd keep having sex until I conceived. The chosen men had an eternal destiny. Those men, Enzo, Gene, Silas, maybe Jeremy, they aren't dead. They're with Dewey now, helping him prepare our eternal home, where they'll serve us forever."

"But where are their bodies, Anna?"

"I discovered that mixing sleeping pills with my allergy medication has a rather tranquilizing effect. All of the men, except Jeremy, were very cooperative when I took them up Mount Olympus. It really is a beautiful place to—"

But before I could finish, police came barreling in, shouting that they needed to see my hands.

It was all very traumatic, my sister's betrayal, my arrest and imprisonment. I don't think I'll be here long, though. Jeremy's in jail. Instead of having a sedating effect, like it did on the others, the cocktail I gave him made him manic. The police found him at the hotel, wearing that creepy mask, and connected him to a series of home robberies in Millcreek. So I'm kind of a heroine, in that regard.

Resha's had time to calm down and see that I was right. She's already told me that she feels terrible for betraying me, partly because she realizes that I was coming to help her but mostly because I'm pregnant with a baby girl. My sister now understands the importance of the *Tablets* and our legacy. She has a brilliant plan to get me out of here. Goddesses stick together.

TERRI BARANOWSKI is a writer, speaker, literary agent, and founder of Gateway Literary. The author of several award-winning humorous essays, Terri served as guest feature columnist for a St. Louis newspaper, co-created an ARG and a never aired television dramedy series, and assisted in the creation of *The Criterion*, Brigham Young University's first literary criticism journal. She resides in Holladay, Utah with two adorable Shih Tzus and is currently working on her first novel, *Academic Affairs: Unleashing the Chimera*, which aspires to be literary fiction if only a few uncooperative characters would stop turning it into chick lit.

You can find Terri at gatewayliterary.com.

A LITTLE NIGHT VISIT

BY JOSHUA P. SORENSEN

Cough!

I jerk awake.

From the apartment below me, *Bump-dah-dup.* I've heard that before, Mozart I think. But the music is not what woke me; I'm used to that.

My downstairs neighbor is a musical savant. Maybe nineteen years old, worldwide fame surrounds him. He plays with true genius, like sell-your-soul-at-the-crossroads-to-learn-guitar talent. But Sebastian Faure has mastered more instruments than just guitar.

You would think having today's preeminent musician in the world living right below you would be a non-stop party.

It is not.

It is musical noise at weird hours, haunting piano melodies drifting up the stairwell, and choruses of strings emanating through the floorboards like the rising dead. You aren't supposed to hear your downstairs neighbor.

Cough! Cough!

Again, the sound that woke me. It's coming from inside my apartment. The floorboards creak in an unsteady rhythm. Someone is walking slowly down my hall.

Cough! Cough! Cough!

The high-pitched squeaks stop right outside my bedroom door. I scrabble around my nightstand in panic. Clicking on the desk lamp, the sudden brightness momentarily blinds me. I turn the light onto the door. Shadows consume the light, giving the room a distorted shape. The door appears distant, as if at the end of a long hallway. My breath frosts.

My door, ever so slowly, creaks open. The whine of the hinge crescendos in a discordant note. A man stands in the illuminated portal. His clothes are odd, ragged, torn, and covered in filth, but even odder than that is the bag he is wearing over his head.

Cough!

A violent cough, yet he doesn't move. Then the smell hits me. Rotting meat mixed with an acrid chemical stench. I cover my face, stifling a gag.

When I look up, the man is standing next to my bed. I didn't see him move. Now, he just stands motionless at my bedside.

I grab my desk lamp and hold it before me like a weapon. The light swings around the room as I try to focus on him. Out of the corner of my eye, I catch another man at my chamber door.

"Sebastian! What is happening? Help me!"

Sebastian stands silent sentinel to the scene. His dead stare seems to glow with an unearthly brilliance.

With a terrible certainty, my attention is pulled inexorably back to the intruder at my bedside. He has removed his bag, emptying gore and lye onto my lap. His face is desiccated.

Sunken black eyes contrast on morbid pale skin. Dried blood stains his nostrils and mouth. His dark stare pierces my soul.

Cough!

I cough, not him. Pressure builds in my chest. My lungs burn.

Cough! Cough!

Blood pours from my sinuses. I try to call to Sebastian. I can't breathe.

Cough! Cough! Cough!

Along with my lifeblood, I can feel my life energy being coughed out. My visitor seems to inhale it; his features enliven with each cough. His skin blushes and the sinews relax into a more natural position. Liveliness returns to his shadowy features. But the odious stench intensifies into a macabre miasma of death.

Sebastian keeps his silent vigil from my doorway.

Cough!

I collapse. I should run, escape, fight, but it is too late. I sense the last of my blood, the last of my soul, the last of me, slip forth into the ether.

Licking his lips, Sebastian orders, "Wolfgang Amadeus! You have his soul, now time to teach me my next lesson."

JOSHUA P. SORENSEN is a retired soldier and graduate of Norwich University. He enjoys writing poetry and short fiction. His other loves include history, nature, and all things geek. He can be found on Facebook: @SorensenVagabondWriter .

THE FORGOTTEN TWIN

BY LAURIE HEATH

"**M**ommy," Carly said, "I want Hailey."

Danielle stopped pushing the shopping cart and stared in disbelief at her three-year-old and then at her husband. He ran his fingers through his deep chestnut hair, and tears welled in his eyes, reflecting the anguish surging through her. Surely their child had picked the name out of thin air, perhaps heard it in daycare.

"You want who?" Danielle's voice barely carried the words across the meager distance between her and her daughter.

"Hailey." Carly's little voice had such conviction. "She's my sister, silly Mommy!"

Carly's teasing laugh sent chills down her mother's spine. Danielle suppressed the urge to slap her little girl across the face.

They had been so careful around Carly. Ever since the charred remains of Carly's twin had been buried, they hadn't mentioned her. How long had it been? Two and a half years, almost to the day. The guilt drowned Danielle's anger. If only she hadn't left Hailey alone while she'd been bathing Carly. Hailey had been asleep. It was only going to be a few minutes—

"Daddy, take me to see toys. Mommy can shop." Carly stretched her hands out to her father.

Was he trying to get the image of their mangled, charred baby out of his mind like she was?

"No, Honey. We're just about finished. We'll look at toys another day."

"Okay, Daddy. We'll look at toys another day. Hailey will come with us! That will be fun, Daddy!"

Jake took over pushing the cart, somehow forcing levity that Danielle couldn't fake. She was lost in the nightmare. It was too vivid. For weeks after Hailey's abduction, Carly had been inconsolable. She knew that the one who had shared womb and crib was gone.

They had never mentioned the baby they lost in Carly's presence, only remembering her in whispers when their surviving child was at daycare or one of their parents was watching her. Every picture of the twins together was hidden in a box in the darkest corner of the bedroom closet on a shelf they both needed a stepstool to reach.

Danielle barely remembered standing in the checkout line, but they had reached the car. Jake lifted Carly out of the shopping cart and buckled her into her car seat.

"Don't forget Hailey." The blonde curls shook as the child nodded her head. "We want Hailey safe too."

Danielle stepped away from the car and took the cart to the cart return. Out of the corner of her eye, she saw Jake fasten the seatbelt beside Carly's car seat. It had to be an imaginary friend. A coincidence. A name she heard at daycare. No one would tell a three-year-old what had happened to her twin sister. No one would be that sadistic.

Danielle and Jake spent the afternoon and evening trying to ignore their daughter, who prattled to the imaginary friend she'd named after her twin. The hard stone of guilt wasn't made any lighter when she left Jake alone with their daughter while she locked herself in the bathroom and cried until she was empty and numb.

Later that night, when their angelic daughter was sleeping, they finally talked.

"It's a coincidence," Jake rationalized.

Danielle knew that's how he managed to hold himself together when she could barely function.

"She probably got the name from a new kid at the daycare. Maybe she's hinting that she wants us to have another baby."

"Or maybe it is an imaginary friend," Danielle tried to convince herself. "Kids her age have imaginary friends. Tomorrow her imaginary friend will have a new name."

Carly didn't forget her imaginary friend the following day or the one after that. If anything, she became more about including her "sister" in all her activities. Carly insisted that Hailey needed to eat next to her.

"Please, Mommy. Look how sad and hungry Hailey looks. I won't eat if she doesn't eat."

"Carly, eat your lunch."

"No, Mommy. I'm sharing with Hailey because you're being a mean, mean Mommy. It's bad of you."

Danielle's throat throbbed and ached from choking back tears and raising her voice at her stubborn toddler. Carly had refused to eat lunch or dinner the day before. "Please eat, Honey. You like Cocoa Puffs. Look, it makes chocolate milk if you eat it all gone." Danielle stirred the cereal. Her hand was shaking. "See? I like Cocoa Puffs too." Danielle chewed a mouthful of cereal.

Carly took a bite. Danielle closed her eyes. Maybe it would be a better day.

Carly threw the bowl. It crashed against a wall, splattering milk and cereal across the kitchen. "Hailey is hungry!" She screamed at the top of her lungs.

"Get out of here!" Danielle screamed, "Go to your room until I say you can come out!"

The tears and sobs made it difficult to clean up the mess. She could hear Carly singing in her room. "Mean Mommy! Mean Mommy!"

Danielle sat against the wall, wet dishrag in hand and milk seeping through her pants. She wasn't sure how much longer she could take this.

Later that night, Jake fixed an extra plate with a small portion of chicken fingers and a large serving of mixed vegetables.

"What are you doing?" Danielle asked, eyeing the plate with suspicion while she rinsed off her own.

"If Hailey wants to eat, we'll let her." He set the plate next to Carly's full one before taking his already empty dish to the sink. "Maybe Hailey likes those mixed vegetables more than Carly," he joked.

"Thanks, Mommy and Daddy." Carly scooted out of her booster seat. "We're going to play now!" She ran out the back door before either of her parents could object.

"I don't believe it." Danielle brought the two empty plates to the sink. "She ate everything. She was starving."

"She hates mixed vegetables. I can't believe she ate all

of them."

"Hailey must have eaten them," Danielle joked, letting the bitterness ooze into the words. Deep inside, she couldn't help but doubt that the child they had to force feed mixed veggies would eat two platefuls. She wasn't sure what to make of her daughter's behavior, but she was relieved she had finally eaten.

Jake and Danielle tried to keep a sense of humor. Everyone told them that tantrums and imaginary friends were a phase every normal, healthy child went through. Their family and neighbors were kinder to them than they were to themselves. They felt guilty for being so angry at their daughter for reminding them of the daughter they had lost.

On Wednesday Danielle picked Carly up from daycare when her teacher, Mrs. Ellie, stopped her.

"Can I have a word with you?"

Danielle turned away from watching her daughter, who was playing alone in a corner with a doll.

"Carly isn't acting like herself." The older woman faltered, momentarily fidgeting with her wedding ring. "Lately she hasn't been eating, she's throwing temper tantrums, she refuses to play with the other kids. Usually she's such a happy, easy-going little girl, but lately—" She rolled up her turquoise sweater; her forearm was swollen and bruised. There were scabs where the skin had broken. It looked like a small animal had sunk its teeth into her arm and wouldn't let go.

"She did that?" Danielle was stunned. Carly had never been a biter. She'd gone through a hitting stage, but she'd never used her teeth on anyone.

"I wouldn't bring it up"—she rolled her sleeve down—"but today she bit three other kids. One of the bites is worse than this. The last couple days she has been scaring the kids with stories about a girl named Hailey. She went so far as to blame the biting on this imaginary friend."

Danielle blinked back the tears, but she couldn't hide the way her cheeks were burning. Why was her daughter acting out? "Is there anything else?" Danielle asked, dreading what the teacher was waiting to tell her.

"She has started talking in her sleep. I've heard her moaning and even arguing in her sleep."

That was something Danielle hadn't noticed, but she had to admit that she'd been rushing bedtime with her daughter since that day in the store. Maybe she was a bad mommy. She vowed to do better, be a more patient, observant mother. Maybe then Carly would love her again. Danielle shook that last thought away. Of course Carly loved her. Didn't she?

"I can't have her here," Mrs. Ellie finally said. "She can come back when she's out of this phase, but when she's hurting other kids, I have to draw the line."

Danielle nodded her head, barely feeling the movement. She had relished the reprieve daycare had given her, but seeing the wound, imagining it on a toddler, she knew the teacher was right.

Carly noticed her mom at that moment. "Mommy!" she exclaimed, dropping the doll she'd been playing with and running to her. She wrapped her tiny arms around Danielle's thighs, rubbing her face against the fabric of her skirt. Danielle automatically stroked her daughter's head; this was just like old Carly.

"Ow!" she exclaimed when she felt teeth piercing her skin through the thin skirt.

"Did she just bite you?" Mrs. Ellie asked, not sounding surprised.

"Hailey told me to." Carly laughed as if it were a grand prank. "She said it would be silly. Silly, bad Mommy!" Carly ran across the room as if to play tag.

Danielle fought back the tears.

"Let's take a look." Mrs. Ellie led Danielle to the story time seat.

Danielle didn't realize how dizzy she felt until she sat down. She raised the hem of her light cotton skirt. She was bleeding from the puncture wounds. The center of the bite was already turning a vibrant purple.

Mrs. Ellie brought the first aid kit over to her and Danielle started cleaning and bandaging the wound. Kids nearby were already talking about how Scary Carly had even dared to bite her mommy. Danielle could hear the fear in their voices. Carly had to get out of there before she could cause anymore fear or harm.

Danielle thanked Mrs. Ellie, scooped up the angelically smiling child, and left without another word.

That night, Danielle fixed an extra plate of lasagna and broccoli smothered in cheese and set it beside Carly. The bite on her thigh throbbed and the thought of sending her daughter into an angry fit made her heart pound against her rib cage and she couldn't hide the tremor in her hands.

Carly ate her dinner with gusto, even the broccoli. She asked for seconds when Jake started clearing dishes from the table.

Danielle cut up a square of lasagna for her daughter. "More brocc'li too," Carly said, taking a large bite of pasta. Danielle spooned the last of the florets on to her plate and took the empty bowl and plate to the dishwasher where Jake was starting to load the dinner dishes.

"Hailey wants more lasagna," Carly called from the table.

Jake looked across the counter to the table. The plate for "Hailey" was empty and Carly was finishing up the broccoli.

"Hungry kid," he commented.

Danielle put the very last of the lasagna on the empty plate. She took the casserole dish to the sink and started filling it with water. As the dish was filling, she looked over at her daughter and saw that, just as Jake had said, the plate next to Carly was empty. Where had the food gone? Carly couldn't have eaten it that fast. She was still eating the broccoli from her own plate like she had been when Danielle had turned her back a moment ago.

Danielle turned off the water and walked over to the table. "Did you eat that lasagna I put on the other plate?" She looked her daughter in the eyes, hoping Carly couldn't see the fear Danielle felt. Hoping it didn't sound like an accusation to the little girl whose chin and cheeks were painted with the pasta sauce.

"Hailey ate her dinner, Mommy. She's a good girl." Carly sounded surprised that her mom didn't know Hailey had polished off her own dinner. "We're going to go play now," Carly said.

"Not with that dirty face," Jake said. "How about a bubble bath instead? You have cheese and sauce up to your elbows!"

"It was yummy. Mommy did a good job. Hailey even said so."

Danielle wasn't sure she if she ought to be flattered an imaginary monster liked her cooking or if she was relieved her daughter hadn't called her "bad Mommy." Those words felt like daggers echoing and tearing at her soul.

"I'll stay home with her tomorrow. My mom couldn't do it,

but she said she could watch her Thursday." Jake said after Carly was tucked into bed.

"It's sad that work feels like a reprieve. Makes me feel guilty," Danielle said, feeling the weight of her secret thoughts easing slightly.

"She's *our* responsibility. I can't believe she bit you. I think it's time we start getting her some help. I have the name of a good child therapist."

Danielle nodded.

They stopped at Carly's bedroom door before going to bed. The child was tangled in her blankets, tossing and turning as if she were having trouble getting comfortable. Short cries and moans escaped her rosebud lips. Danielle wanted to straighten the blankets, brush back the hair that plastered against her cherubic face, take away whatever bad dreams plagued her. She didn't dare wake her.

———

JAKE CALLED Danielle at work just as she was leaving for lunch.

"We're going to Primary Children's Hospital. Meet us there." His voice sounded strained, trembling. He hung up before Danielle could ask him what had happened. She told the receptionist there was an emergency and asked her to let people know she wouldn't be back that day as she ran out the door.

She fumbled with her keys. Dropped them. Picked them up. She crouched against her car, holding on to it for support. Hailey's tiny charred body, her glassy eyes staring at the sky. For a moment, she was in that field where Hailey had been found. No. Jake wouldn't let it happen. What could have happened?

Danielle arrived at Primary Children's emergency room in time to see a stretcher with the tiny body of her daughter strapped to it. A blood-soaked bandage plastered Carly's head. She was shrieking so loudly no other conversation could be heard. Jake hopped out slowly, as if he was too shaky to stand on his own.

"What happened? What happened?" Danielle screamed, trying to make herself heard.

He only shook his head, unable to form words. Jake was talkative. He always knew what to say. This was bad. Really bad. Hailey's tiny body flashed in her mind. No. Not again.

"Stay here," a nurse told them outside of the partitioned area where their daughter was wheeled. "The doctors need room to work."

"What happened?" Danielle asked again. Their daughter wasn't crying anymore. The nurse let them into the room. Carly's tiny body seemed too tiny to have so many wires and tubes attached to it. She was too still. Only the regular beeping from the heart monitor assured Danielle that she was still alive but had been sedated.

Jake was hoarse when he spoke. "I-I'm sorry. I fixed lunch. I put her bowl in front of her and then I went to grab my bowl of soup." He gulped and ran his hand through his short hair. "I turned away from her for just a moment. The next thing I knew —oh God. It was awful. She was pushing the handle of her spoon into her eye, digging at it."

A sour taste filled Danielle's mouth. She was dizzy, her stomach roiled. This couldn't be happening. She barely made it to a wastebasket before she threw up.

A specialist assessed Carly's condition and soon she was in surgery. What could've compelled their daughter to do something so horrible to herself? They mindlessly thumbed through tattered magazines, most as old as their daughter. They drank bitter hours-old coffee, but neither of them tasted it. It was something to kill the interminably long wait while their daughter was in the operating room.

The surgeon came out. A blue mask dangled from his neck. The bags under his eyes made him seem older, exhausted. Sweat still glistened on his forehead. "Mr. and Mrs. Titus?" he called out, trying to decide which cluster of people he needed to address. Jake and Danielle stood up and went to the surgeon.

"There was too much damage to her eye. I couldn't save it." After a pause to let the news sink in he continued. "Once her eye socket is fully healed, she can be fitted for a prosthetic. She needs to stay here at least overnight for observation. I'll come by tomorrow morning and we can discuss what happens next. She'll be asleep for a while longer." The surgeon wiped a bead of sweat from his forehead with his forearm, "For a toddler she was difficult to sedate and keep sedated during the procedure. She'll be moved to a private room soon."

Carly was tiny in the hospital bed. Half her pale face was covered with gauze. An IV and heart rate monitor were taped to her left arm. She was so still that her parents couldn't see her breathing. If the monitor wasn't showing that she had a pulse, they would have thought the worst.

She stirred. Her good eye fluttered, trying to shake off the anesthetic sleep. She turned her head towards her parents. "Hailey did it," she said before she resumed her drug-induced sleep.

Danielle received an extended leave from work. Carly was in the hospital for two long days and Danielle didn't leave her daughter's side. During her stay, Carly was almost a normal toddler, except quieter. She spent her time coloring in the coloring books her parents and grandparents brought her and snuggling with a large teddy bear Danielle and Jake brought to her room after surgery.

A child psychologist and a social worker visited their room daily, interviewing both parents, talking to Carly as well. The conclusion was the child hadn't been abused and she seemed like any normal child.

"Here's my card," the child psychologist said. "Make an appointment if her behavior regresses. Until then, she seems like a normal little girl who had a bad accident."

They had their Carly back. She hadn't mentioned Hailey and she acted as if being blind in one eye was normal.

———

THREE MONTHS later Carly had a prosthetic eye that replaced the pink eye patch and bandage. It almost looked like her other dark blue eye. Occasionally a shadow darkened Carley's bright face and everything inside Danielle tightened like a noose, but it passed as quickly as it appeared.

One night at bedtime the family was gathered in Carly's room. Jake read a new storybook he had bought for Carly, *The Ugly Duckling*. At the end, the ugly little duckling transformed into a magnificent swan. Carly's sigh surprised her parents. "Hailey wishes she would turn into a beautiful little girl. Hailey doesn't like her burnt body and her crooked neck. She wants to be like the swan, Mommy and Daddy." A tear ran down her cheek.

Danielle's hand rose to her mouth. She bit her finger, choking an anguished cry. How did Carly know? The image was grotesque; it didn't belong in a little girl's imagination. They kissed her goodnight and left her alone.

In the early hours of the morning, screams startled Danielle and Jake awake. They ran, stumbling into Carly's room. The room looked like a fire had charred everything. Books were piles of ashes; stuffed animals and dolls were transformed into hard plastic mounds. There was no smoke, not even the smell of anything burning. Carly sat in the center of what remained of her bed. Her favorite red pajamas were black and falling off her. She didn't look hurt.

"Hailey wanted my things to look like hers." A haunted look made her look centuries older than three. "I screamed 'cause she made it too hot."

Carly slept between them for several days while her room was cleaned and repaired by Utah Disaster Kleenup. Danielle held Carly close to her, just like she had when Carly was a baby, after Hailey's death. She needed to protect Carly, prove to herself and her child that she wasn't a bad mommy.

Days later, Danielle crawled around the remodeled room, filled with a new bed and bedding, toys, and clothes. "Carly, do you want to play with your new Barbies? We can make them a Lego house." Danielle was growing weary of trying to engage her daughter and be her friend, but thinking of how close she had been to losing her compelled her to keep trying.

"Hailey hates these new things!" Carly tore the sheets off the bed. The dark expression on Carly's face made Danielle shudder.

Danielle closed the door. She *was* a bad mommy. She couldn't control her own daughter. She couldn't make her daughter happy. Worse, Danielle was terrified of her.

Two hours later when Danielle dared open Carly's bedroom

door, she saw new dolls with their heads and limbs ripped from their bodies. The bedding was shredded. The freshly painted walls had images drawn in black and red depicting in crude form the torture of a small stick figure by larger stick figures. Carly was sprawled on the floor, still clutching the stub of red crayon.

At bedtime, the frightened little girl curled up between her parents in their bed.

"I made an appointment with that child psychologist," Jake said. "You've changed. You're scared of your own shadow. You're crying a lot. And honestly, she scares me as well."

Danielle felt her heart beat faster. It was the best news she had heard in weeks. "When is the appointment?"

"Four months away. That's the soonest appointment. But she's the best in the state."

"That's not too far away," Danielle said, more to reassure herself. She could make it a few months. She'd just need to work harder to be a good mommy. A mommy that Carly would love so she wouldn't throw tantrums. She squeezed her sleeping child, perhaps too tight because she thought she heard Carly whisper, "Mean Mommy."

Carly's temper increased. Macabre drawings decorated chairs, walls throughout the house, even the television. Jake and Danielle tried to restrain Carly during the worst of her tantrums, only to receive bites that tore chunks from their flesh. Carly threw food out of the refrigerator. She threw fresh eggs on the furniture and carpet, grinding the egg yolk into the fabric. Milk and juice were poured on the floor. All of this done with silent maliciousness.

Danielle no longer begged Carly to stop drawing on the furniture or emptying the contents of the fridge onto the floors.

She sat paralyzed on the couch each day, watching Food Network with the volume loud enough to drown out the destruction her daughter was wreaking. She was losing the battle and there was no sense in fighting.

Four months more. Would there be anything left of her sanity?

By the end of a weekend that felt longer than it was—an antique lamp had been thrown hard enough it had left a hole in the wall—they lost the last of their patience. Danielle and Jake had deep bite marks on top of older bite marks. Their child's mocking laughs with each new attack only made it worse. "Bad Mommy, Bad Daddy! Carly and Hailey hate you! Bad Mommy. Bad Daddy!" she would scream in a sing-song voice.

Jake locked Carly in her room. Danielle was too exhausted to object or do anything else. She leaned against Jake on the marker and egg stained sofa. "We need to get her help. The accident led us to believe she was okay. She isn't." Danielle could feel Jake's body shaking involuntarily, like her own. He had a small hand-shaped welt on his cheek.

"They would want to keep her forever. We can't just lock her up and throw away the key."

"We wouldn't. Jake, she isn't safe here. We're not safe. She needs help now, not in a few months."

"You're not putting me in a nut house," Carly exclaimed. She was standing in front of them. How? A jump rope had been tied from her doorknob to the bathroom door. When Danielle peeked around the corner, she saw the rope frayed and hanging limp from her wide-open bedroom. Had she chewed through the rope? How could she have gotten her head through the door? It had been secure. She looked at the rope in disbelief. She didn't know how it had happened. Maybe she was going crazy.

"Bad Mommy and Daddy! Don't you want your precious baby girl?" Carly was screaming as she ran into the kitchen. How did she know those words? Where had she learned to use such a venomous tone? Something inside Danielle snapped. The paralysis and silence that had held her captive disappeared, and she was ready to show her daughter who was in charge. If Carly could dish it out, she could take what was coming.

Before Danielle could catch her and shake some sense into her, Carly ran full speed and crashed into the glass center of the backdoor. She hit with impossible force, sending shards of glass crashing and cascading down around her.

"Carly!" Danielle screamed as she ran through the broken glass door, not minding how the knife-like fragments that remained cleaving to the door tore her skin, forgetting the rage that had impelled her forward. "Carly!"

She lay in the grass beyond the door. She had hit with such force that it had carried her past the tiny patio and into the grass. Tiny cuts glinted in the light, reflecting blood and glass. Deep gashes shone ruby red in the sunlight. Not a limb or area on her body was free from the cuts, the fragments of glass.

Danielle knelt beside the crumpled, broken body, Jake at her side. Dazed, she shook her head. No. Not her baby. Not again.

Carly was still. Too still. Her ear nearly touched her shoulder at a frightening angle. A stream of blood seeped from a severed vein in her neck. Nothing could be done now.

Danielle stared at the broken, lifeless body for so long. She held one tiny bloody hand. Jake held the other. Her eyes were too blurred with tears to see anything with clarity. Only a bad mother would lose two babies in such terrible ways. If only she could have another chance.

Blinking away the tears, an optical illusion occurred: the

wounds were closing. Danielle turned away and when she looked again, the gashes were thin surface scratches.

The child moved her head out of the uncomfortable position. Her eyes fluttered open. Two beautiful brown eyes stared up at her astounded parents.

"Oh, Carly," whispered Danielle.

The child sat up, cracked her neck by pressing her hand against her head and tilting it to the side, and smiled darkly. "I'm Hailey."

LAURIE HEATH has been writing short stories since she was 14. She hasn't met a fabric craft she dislikes, but her favorite is knitting. She currently lives in West Valley City, Utah with her partner, Craig, and their cats, Mystery and Mayhem.

MORSEL

BY JO SCHNEIDER

The hunger comes when I'm sleeping. Dull at first, interrupting my dreams and twisting them into disturbing visions of death. Death that I long for but cannot have.

I wake growling. Straining against the leather strips that anchor my hands behind the pole that rises from the cold cement floor. The cool metal burns between my shoulder blades. I'm surprised my skeletal arms don't snap as I struggle.

Darkness surrounds me, sinks into me. It is broken only by a dull gray line around the nearby garage door.

The others are quiet. Sleeping. Lucky them. They haven't been here long enough to have given up and to then realize that any escape is a fantasy.

They sit on the ground, their arms tied around the poles behind them. I am on my knees, my ankles tied behind me. My captors were irked when I tried to feed on myself. They even bandaged the place where I took a chunk out of my thigh. They don't want to share.

Only three have gone before me. Not dead. Not alive. All I

know is they're not here anymore, and their screams echoed for days.

Twilight bleeds into night. I can feel it in my flesh. My bones. I can smell it like the scent of leaves before rain.

I double over, my stomach compressing, searching for something to digest. It only finds itself. I wonder if I should be as optimistic as my stomach is. Not having a brain must be nice.

A click sounds from my right.

I straighten and hold my breath. The air stills as the others hold theirs, too. Cold sweeps in as the door to the garage opens.

Every muscle in my body freezes. Each hair on my arms comes to attention. Gray spills in from outside, outlining the shadow of what looks like a man.

The starlight glints off my chest. A name tag—my name tag—is all that remains of my old life. It clings courageously to the tatters of the orange blouse that I wore to work at the diner. This is as much as I can remember, and even that only comes in flashes—clinking silverware, dark smooth color of coffee, the smell of roast beef.

The door closes and the glimmer of the past fades.

Footsteps approach. A few of the others whimper, but I know he's coming for me. My breath comes in ragged gasps, matching the cadence of his walk.

I've never seen his face, but I have tasted his hot breath and felt his weathered hands.

The thumping of his boots stops, and he squats down. The scent of decay settles around me.

He never speaks. I've long since stopped begging for my life, for the reason why I'm here. I think he savors my silence.

I jump as a hand, large and cool, strokes my neck. His fingers rub over the circle of wounds there. Caressing them. His breathing becomes heavier, and his hand moves to the back of my head. His fingers push into and grab my long, matted hair, then he gently arches my body back until I stare at the darkness above.

I squeeze my eyes shut and try to calm my trembling body. If not for my skin, I would have already exploded. I shudder as his tongue licks each wound, reopening them.

He moans. The only sound he ever makes. A shudder runs through me and I gasp as he sinks his teeth into my neck.

His free hand rubs my back as if comforting me. Warmth rises to my neck and I feel the blood drawn out of me as if through a straw.

It should hurt, but it doesn't. It never has. Instead, a shiver of delight runs through me.

I've learned not to move. If I move, he'll pull away before he's finished. I don't want that. So, I wait.

He takes his time. I can tell when he's almost finished because he begins licking the punctures again. They seal, and he moves away a little.

I'm breathing hard and fast, shaking as if from cold. I take a breath, but stop myself. Asking doesn't work.

He remains next to me for a long time. Long enough that I slump, exhausted after just a few minutes of being awake. I let my head fall forward and I'm glad I can't produce tears.

I cry out when his hand grabs my hair and yanks it back. Something slick and warm presses against my mouth. I part my lips as he slips something inside.

Raw meat.

I want to spit it out, but it's the only food I've had in days, and I swallow like a greedy dog. Then, without meaning to, I open my mouth. To my surprise, he gives me more. As I gobble it down, he leans close. His lips brush my ear as he speaks for the first time. His voice is deep and smooth. "Next time will be the last."

He lets go of my hair and I slump forward, my stomach already anticipating what's to come.

I want to vomit, but won't let myself.

The garage door closes with a thump. The others begin to whimper.

His words echo in my head, and I sob.

JO SCHNEIDER grew up in the wild west, and finds mountains helpful in telling which direction she is going. Her lifelong goals include: travel to all seven continents, become a Jedi Knight and receive a death threat from a fan. So far she's been to five continents, has a black belt in Kempo and is still working on the death threat. Being a geek at heart, Jo has always been drawn to science fiction, fantasy and horror. She hopes to introduce readers to worlds that wow them and characters they can cheer for.

PREDATOR

BY MATTHEW CORNACHIONE

Fur this beautiful begged to be petted. Even with her background, Kim had to restrain herself. It wouldn't do to break protocol on the first open tour of the Rocky Mountain Predator Research Center.

And petting a coyote was a great way to lose some skin.

Kim gave one last backward look at the beautiful specimen. Wide yellow eyes stared back. They blinked, highlighting a scar over the left eye. She almost convinced herself that it was wishing her farewell. In reality, it was probably deciding if she was a threat or a target. Kim hustled after the tour group.

"As you can see, we have eight wolves in this section. That gives us the largest collection of these animals in the Rocky Mountains. We are better poised to study their physiology and behavior than anyone in the world."

That was Rebecca Wilkins, the head of the Predator Research Center, or the PRC as it was usually known. She kept a tight lid on the goings-on at her facility but had finally granted access to a limited tour. Kim was one of a dozen canid researchers, all eager to see what was happening behind these doors.

On the left was a massive cage with several gray wolves inside. Kim didn't count eight, but there were a couple hiding places. These were bigger than the coyotes, and darker too. They stirred as the group passed, unusually restless. In these animals, Kim was hard pressed to imagine any friendliness. There was a calculated intelligence behind those eyes and a complete lack of fear.

"We are beginning a breeding program this year with the intent to grow our numbers and allow for—"

"For more animal abuse." A voice in the crowd cut Rebecca off.

Kim's breath caught. She didn't recognize the voice, but she knew the rhetoric. That had to be James Olson of the North American Wolf Foundation. His crusade against the PRC had been public and vocal for years. Rebecca glared into the group, obviously affronted.

"Nonsense. All of the animals here are treated with the utmost care and respect."

A wiry man in his early fifties pushed to the front. "I know what your website says. But what I see is an animal prison. These cages are much too small for these proud animals. Wolves and coyotes need to range free."

"Our country already tried that, if you recall. Wolves all but vanished while coyote numbers surged. What we need is informed science to create intelligent population management. Whether you like it or not, work done at this facility is crucial to a peaceful coexistence between humans and wild canids."

"You're so full of yourself. The same thing can be accomplished by observing wolves in situ. The PRC only makes—"

"Enough. We can continue this *discussion* after the tour. I'm sure everyone else is eager to see the monitoring center."

Murmurs of assent rippled through the group. Kim found herself nodding, all too happy to avoid a shouting match. Besides, the monitoring center was her main interest.

James muttered under his breath, but, thankfully, backed down. The rest of the researchers followed Rebecca as she resumed her tour, as if nothing had happened.

By the far end of the wolf enclosure was a door leading back into the main complex. Kim followed everyone through. The interior was even more impressive than she'd expected. Hosts of computer screens bedecked the walls showing feeds from the wolf and coyote pens. They had multiple camera angles, including infrared which revealed the hidden wolves. Other screens showed running graphs with readouts of heart rate and oxygen saturation. Everything that could be measured, was.

At the center of it all was a PRC scientist manning a computer terminal. Rebecca strode over to him and addressed the visiting researchers.

"This is our pride and joy, the monitoring center. Here we track animal health and well-being in real time. GPS readouts record animal movement patterns. We can figure out exactly how far these animals walk every day, what path they take, and how hard they worked to get there. In the holding pens behind us," Rebecca gestured over her shoulder to an open door, "we perform monthly physicals. Here we can assess the wolf and coyote responses to different stimuli, changes in diet, and anything else you can imagine. All that we learn passes through this single room."

Kim was in awe. It was rare to catch a glimpse of a wolf and even rarer to find it doing anything interesting. To have this much information... well that would be a godsend. The PRC was extremely well equipped.

"You may have noticed that the animals are especially agitated today. We're a couple of weeks into to our latest project. This study will identify changes in social dynamics and pack behavior under drought conditions."

As Rebecca spoke, Kim scanned the room. She might never get to come here again so she took it all in. The brilliant monitors, the blood sample testing equipment, the crisp clean décor. So amazing.

"So, basically you're starving them." James made no effort to hide his anger.

"Not at all. Each animal is given sufficient calories to survive. However, yes, you could say they are a little hungry. The rule here is 'never turn your back on a wolf.' In this condition, I wouldn't even turn my back on a coyote."

Kim caught sight of something odd on a monitor. One of the gates to the coyote pen rolled aside. The animals stirred, staring into the opening. Kim checked the other monitors and saw the same thing was happening in the wolf enclosure. Was this some kind of demonstration?

"You're just confirming everything I've said. This facility is nothing but a torture chamber."

Kim raised her hand. "Excuse me, but are the cages supposed to be opening?"

Rebecca closed her mouth, swallowing her reply to James. Her brow furrowed and she checked the monitors. "What's going on?" she asked her lead scientist.

He typed furiously. Kim's gut was roiling. Something was obviously wrong. The scientist shook his head.

"Sound the alarm. Put the facility on lock-down," said

Rebecca. Turning to the researchers, "I'm sorry folks. Just having a little technical difficulty with the gate control systems. We're going to have to move to the front evacuation point."

An alarm blared. Kim jumped. The sound grated down to her very core. *Evacuation point*? That couldn't be good.

The lights cut out and in a moment were replaced with

red lights flashing in time with the alarm. The blinking lights cast the room into a creepy glow. The effect was disorienting and Kim felt herself growing faint. The rest of the researchers broke into nervous chatter.

"Folks." Rebecca's sharp voice cut through the confusion. "Turn around now. Just follow the lighted exit signs and all will be fine. Now go."

A growl echoed from the holding pens.

Kim froze.

There was no mistaking that noise. It was the sound of a predator issuing a threat. A wolf. And there were no doors between it and the researchers.

Someone screamed and the crowd's composure vanished as a wolf entered the hall behind Rebecca.

People ran. Someone slammed into Kim and knocked her to the floor. Whoever it was didn't stop to help her up, but just took off toward the nearest door.

Claws clacked on the concrete and a second wolf growled.

Then came another scream, this one laced not with fear, but with pain.

More people shouted, doors opened and shut. And through it all Kim could only summon the strength to watch. Panic had cut in too fast to comprehend. She caught brief glimpses of chaos through the blinking red alarm. Everyone was scrambling wildly and short dark shapes mixed with the crowd.

Finally, Kim's survival instinct cut through the confusion. She needed to get out of here. She rolled over and pushed to her knees. On the back wall she spotted a friendly green exit sign above a door. She ran for it.

Just before she reached it, a large shape barreled into the door. Kim screamed. Then the red light flashed and she saw it was a man, not a wolf. She pushed through behind him. The pair tumbled out into an open hallway.

It was dim, but a few emergency lights gave enough illumination for guidance. Another exit sign was at one end of the hall. Kim grabbed the man's arm and tugged him toward safety.

The man grunted, then slipped to a knee. "I can't."

Kim recognized the voice: James Olson. She squinted in the weak light and saw a tear in his pants. Blood welled from a jagged wound.

"Yes you can. Come on, let's find a bandage." Kim helped him to stand. He gave her some of his weight and the two limped forward.

Screams and growls sounded from behind them, but no one else made it into the corridor. Kim kept pushing forward, thankful that James was a small man. She knew he was seriously hurt. Without a bandage soon, he might not make it.

Kim found a door and pushed it open. The pair fell into an office. The room was dark but light shone from a laptop sitting on the desk. The owner must have taken off in a hurry when the alarm sounded.

"Sit down." Kim eased James into the padded chair. She glanced around the room for any sort of bandage, but she couldn't see much, let alone an emergency kit. In her own office building, Kim knew there was a first aid kit in the break room. There was a pretty good bet that was true here.

"I'm going to find a first aid kit. Stay here."

"Like I have any choice."

"It'll be okay." Kim was far from sure of that, but what else could she say?

Taking a deep breath, Kim stepped back into the corridor. It was still empty. The screams in the other room had faded, though she still heard footsteps echoing through the halls. Other survivors were out there, but they were now dispersed. With any luck she would find help on the way to the break room.

She shut the door behind her. James would be safe for now. Finding the first aid kit was the bigger challenge. Kim didn't know the building so she guessed and headed out. Break rooms were usually in a central location. She took a likely branch in the corridor and sure enough, there was a double door opening into a large room with a table and refrigerator. An emergency light shone on the wall and beneath it, a first aid kit. Thank goodness.

As she pulled down the first aid kit, there came another scream. Then more clattering of claws. The animals were loose. She couldn't count on finding more help.

She ran for the office where James waited. Claws clattered along the hall behind her. Then she felt the happy touch of the door handle and ducked inside the office, slamming the door closed.

The clattering ran on by. Kim put a hand to her heart and bent over. Researching wolves was one thing, but running from them was completely different. Now she knew how their prey felt.

"Is that you?" James grunted.

"Yes, and I've got a first aid kit. I'll get you patched up."

Kim rifled through the kit in the blue computer light, trying to find a good wrap. Then a light came on. She looked up to see James holding out his cell phone.

"Thought it might help."

"Yes, thanks." That was a good sign. Her companion had his wits about him.

With the light, Kim easily found the right equipment. She cut away the torn section of James' pants, then wiped off the blood as best she could. Beneath it was a clear bite mark. Kim winced, but once the blood was gone, the wound didn't look too deep. James would be just fine.

She smeared on some antiseptic cream, then wrapped a length of gauze around his calf. James groaned, but kept the light steady. Kim taped the end of the wrap and stood up. James settled into his chair.

She peered out the tiny window on the door. She couldn't see anything in the hall. She wanted to get out of this place, but at the same time, they were safe here. Wolves and coyotes couldn't open doors.

That gave her time to think. Time to puzzle through the chaos that had beset them. It was strange. Somehow the whole system had malfunctioned and let the wolves into the monitoring center. But even then, the attack was odd.

Kim thought aloud. "Wolves don't usually come after people. Especially not in superior numbers."

"You heard Rebecca. They're starving the poor animals. Those wolves are so desperate they'll risk anything for a meal. Besides, these ones are acclimated to humans. They don't know us as a threat. That's the problem with captive animals. There's no telling what they're capable of."

Kim had no answer to that. She pursed her lips and scanned back out the window.

"You know she did this," said James.

"What?" Kim turned, confused.

"Rebecca. She staged this whole disaster. Probably trying to take me out. Her only real opposition, right here. She couldn't pass up the opportunity. Let the wolves have him. So what if they hurt someone else. Just like her."

"That doesn't make any sense. She was in there too. I saw it all, she was as surprised as the rest of us. I'm sure this is just an accident."

"Ha! So naive. Fine, go ahead and believe what you want. But let me ask you this. Who has controls to the entire building? Who else could open the gates and kill the power?"

Kim shuddered. James was a sour man, but he had a point. The timing was too coincidental to be an accident. But Kim couldn't believe it was Rebecca. Rebecca was known in the community for her care and commitment to science.

"Okay, maybe it's not an accident. But still, it couldn't be her. This is going to be a huge black mark on her facility. It'll set her research back years, or just shut her down for good. Plus she had no way to guarantee you'd get hurt."

"Huh. An inside job you think? Someone on her crew trying to take the PRC down? I'd shake their hand if it wasn't for this." He gestured to his bloody gauze.

Kim didn't know how to respond to that. Was James so opposed to the PRC that he would condone sabotage? Kim had her convictions, but she wasn't a fanatic.

She busied herself by looking out the window. She didn't want to talk to him anymore. This way at least she could see what was happening. Maybe if someone else came by she could help them take refuge here.

Something rustled behind her. On high alert, she glanced at

James. His flashlight was off, but the light of the computer showed her enough—he snatched something from the side of the laptop. A thumb drive.

Kim's eyes narrowed. "What was that?"

"Nothing."

"What are you doing?"

"I told you. Nothing. I'm just sitting here in pain. Leave me alone."

Kim's blood went cold. Before she could catch herself, she blurted out her thoughts. "It was you."

"Now you are talking crazy."

"You're stealing her files, aren't you?"

James stayed silent. Confirmation enough for Kim. But what could she do about it? Even injured, he was stronger than she. And if he really had sabotaged this facility, she had no idea what he was capable of. Suddenly she realized the danger was much greater than she'd thought.

"Just stay quiet and it'll all be okay. Don't tell anyone and nothing needs to happen to you." James spoke in a soft voice.

"I... I won't say anything."

"Ah, now I don't believe you. You know," James pushed to his feet as he talked, "I never wanted anyone to get hurt. I'm just capitalizing on an opportunity."

He walked toward her, a hand on the desk. "You need to understand that. If you spread falsehoods you'll be doing Rebecca's work. I just can't risk that."

He lunged for her.

Kim screamed and pulled open the door. He would have grabbed her but his leg gave out and he fell. Still, he grasped at her jeans. Kim tore them away and dashed into the hall. She ran back the only way she knew, toward the break room.

Glancing behind, she saw James stagger through the door, steadying himself on the frame. He lurched after her, then stopped, eyes wide. Kim saw what he had seen: a pack of coyotes.

Normally, coyotes kept their distance. These were anything but normal. They charged.

Kim pressed herself to the wall. They ran past her after James. The blood must have drawn them to him. He hustled away, faster than she would have expected with his injury. The coyotes took off after him.

Kim moved forward, but a lone coyote blocked her path. It inched toward her, hackles risen, teeth bared. Kim backed up as it kept coming. She wanted to run, but knew she wouldn't make it.

Her researcher brain kicked in. Coyotes were small animals and rarely attacked grown humans. Nature made the creature hesitant to attack. She just had to give it a little extra push in this weird situation.

So Kim growled.

The animal paused.

She stood tall then, took a step forward, and let out her best roar. She bared her teeth, spread her arms, and did all she could to look dangerous.

It worked. The coyote edged back. Its hackles fell and it tucked its tail. Kim had shown her dominance. When it hung its head, she saw the scar over its left eye. This was the same coyote she'd seen on the tour. She smiled to herself. Maybe it was friendly after all.

One victory, but she wasn't out of this yet. She was still trapped in a dark facility with wolves, coyotes, and an injured maniac on the loose. If it wasn't for James, she would have holed up in another office, but now she needed to get all the way outside, find her car and leave this mess behind.

She headed for the main exit. As she did, the coyote followed her. Strange behavior, but it seemed it had attached itself to her. Fine. It didn't look like it was going to attack her.

Before she reached the end of the corridor, the coyote whined. It backed up, eyes fixed on the corner. Something told her to trust the coyote's instincts.

Kim backed up with the coyote all the way to the next branch. There they waited. There came the telltale clacking on the floor. Something was coming down the hall and Kim had a feeling it wasn't another coyote.

She fled. Kim and the coyote passed the break room and continued across the dim building. There were several exits; Kim was sure she could find another.

At the next branch, she paused and looked both ways. The coyote strode out ahead, seemingly unafraid.

"Thank you, Cotè." It was strange to name a wild animal, but the coyote had just saved Kim's life. Cotè had earned a name.

Kim and Cotè moved deeper through the maze of office corridors until they found another exit sign. She was almost there when a shot blasted from nearby. Without thinking, Kim pushed through the closest door.

She found herself back in the octagonal monitoring room. Somehow she'd gotten turned around. She was no closer to safety, and worse, James had found a gun.

Panic threatened again. Kim needed to keep herself under control. She huddled down and slid under a desk, hoping it would hide her if James came past. The blinking red lights didn't penetrate much down here.

Cotè slipped in and curled up beside her. The coyote seemed unaware of the danger. One part of her wanted to criticize the animal's stupidity, but other part of her was comforted. Cotè seemed to be telling her it was all going to be okay. As terrifying as this was, she had a companion to share it with.

Kim calmed down a little and thought through her options. She could run, but that was risky. Wolves seemed to be everywhere and with a gun James was lethal. Add that to the fact that this facility was hard to navigate and it was really a bad idea. The longer she roamed the halls, the better chance she would come across something she couldn't handle.

She should hide, but she needed to find a spot James couldn't reach. Or a door that locked. That couldn't be too hard, could it? Besides, the PRC was only a few miles from town. Police would be here any minute.

Cotè growled. Something was coming.

Kim peered out and saw dark furry legs nearing her desk. Her options had just disappeared.

Cotè bolted. The wolf snapped at him, but the coyote was quick. It slipped past the wolf and ran out into the dark. So much for her helper.

Kim rolled out and dashed the other way. The wolf swung around and cut her off. It snarled and advanced. Kim raised her arms and growled back but this time her foe was undeterred.

The wolf stalked closer.

Kim backed against a wall.

The wolf pounced.

She dodged to the side. Claws raked her jeans, but the teeth missed. She stumbled and the wolf leaped atop her. Frantic, Kim swung her arms wildly. Jaws snapped in front of her face.

Then she got lucky.

Her elbow connected with the wolf's throat. The animal backed off and gave a little cough. Kim pressed her advantage and popped it on the nose. The attack was weak, but it was more than the wolf could handle. It darted off.

Kim rolled over and bumped into something soft. She touched it and felt linen pants under her fingers. The leg inside was warm, but unmoving. Someone was unconscious. Or worse.

Patting up the leg and torso, Kim felt her way up to the neck for a pulse. She didn't have to go that far. At the chest she touched something wet, sticky, and warm.

Blood.

Her already stressed system finally gave up. Kim hurled up her lunch on the floor. It would probably attract the wolves, but she couldn't stop herself. She sat there on her knees for long seconds until there was nothing left in her poor stomach.

She sat back on her heels. Her cheeks were wet. When had she started crying? How could anyone handle this? At this point, she wondered if she'd be joining the body soon.

Despite her fear, Kim couldn't fight her curiosity. She had to see if this was anyone she recognized. The body was twisted on its side. Kim pushed it over. Even through the dim light, she knew the figure.

James Olson.

Kim didn't believe it, but sure enough there was her bandage, wrapped around his leg. The coyotes must have gotten him after all. Except that his chest wound was unusual for a coyote attack.

"Oh poor girl."

Kim spun around to see Rebecca standing there. In the next blink a flash shone off something in her hand. A gun.

"It *was* you."

"Of course. No one can penetrate our security system."

"But all of the other researchers. So many dead. Why?"

"Don't be melodramatic. A couple may have gotten run down, but most of them are already evacuated to the parking lot. This was never about them."

"So you wanted to kill James? But this will ruin your facility. It's not worth it."

"Oh, quite the opposite. This will give us sympathy from the public and our donors. Plus it'll get the activists off our back for good. Radical James Olson stages a breakout at the PRC. Risks researchers lives to free the animals and steal our data. Not a hard sell. After all, you saw him download some files."

"How did you—"

"That laptop was set up to monitor everything. We recorded your entire conversation and all of James' supposed theft. Enough to convince anyone who asks."

"But you shot him."

"Of course. Had to be sure. Self-defense, aiming for a wolf. I'll figure out something. You're a little tougher sell, but I'll manage."

Rebecca raised the gun.

"Wait! I haven't done anything to you. Please."

"You're just like the rest of them. Meek and timid. Not cut out for this job. To research predators, to really understand them, you have to think like them. You have to feel their hunger, their urges. Their need to kill. I know more about these creatures than you ever will."

In the next blink of light, Kim caught a hint of movement. Atop a desk behind Rebecca was Cotè, slowly stalking the PRC leader.

Kim smiled bitterly. "I know more than you think."

"Whatever. Enjoy your last moment."

The gun fired. Cotè leaped.

———

THE WIND FELT good in his fur. It was like nothing he'd felt before. A true mountain breeze. Cotè looked back across the field to the human lights, to the place of the Keeper. With the help of his true Master, Cotè had killed the Keeper and earned his freedom. The Master's sacrifice would not be forgotten. He tilted his head back and let out a howl in her honor. Then Cotè darted into the trees. It was time to learn the wilds. It was time to hunt.

MATTHEW CORNACHIONE is a PhD student at the University of Utah. He currently studies astrophysics and, though he usually writes science fiction, occasionally dabbles in horror. When he's not writing or studying he enjoys a hike or bike ride with his wife, daughter, and husky. He also loves to read, cook, play video games, and play soccer. He hopes you've enjoyed this story. He'll have more works coming out soon. You can check everything out at his website, www.cornachionetales.com, and follow him on Twitter and Facebook.

TRUTH OR DARE

BY EDWARD MATTHEWS

Douglas looked around with mixed nervousness and excitement. He had never been in the old utility shed behind the school. He had always heard the stories of kids going in there to smoke or do whatever else high schoolers do in forbidden places. But that world was unfamiliar to him. He was much more at home with computer games and fantasy novels. This was new territory.

But it was territory with which Amy, to his surprise, was quite familiar. She made quick work of the padlock securing the door. This was a safeguard put in place after the stories of the teenage indiscretions had made their way to the school administration. He did not see how she did it, but Amy popped the door right open and hurried him inside.

It had been her idea to come here. She approached him right after lunch and told him to wait for her in front of the school after his last class. He had smiled dumbly at her, about all he could usually muster when she spoke to him. He was, at least, able to tell her that he would be there.

He could not concentrate in his classes that afternoon and spent the next two-and-a-half hours sweating and wondering what possible reason she could have for wanting to see him. After the bell, he had hurried outside and found her at the front entrance. They had lingered there until most everyone had gone, then snuck together around the back.

Now, standing just inside the entrance of the shed, he still could not understand why she asked him here. He had known her for a long time, but they weren't really friends. They had been in school together for nine years, since the second grade. They had shared some classes and talked now and again. He had always thought she was cute. He had a crush on her for the past four years, but, if anything, this had dampened their relationship. It had made him afraid to talk to her. Their interactions usually began in some awkward exchange of syllables and ended with him averting his eyes and walking away. But here he was, behind the school in the forbidden shed with her.

Douglas looked around the dimly lit space. He saw an assortment of tools, lawn care equipment, and what he assumed were bags of fertilizer or weed killer. There was a small workbench in the back cluttered with sprinkler parts and other bits and pieces from unfinished projects. A few spider webs hung around the windows, but generally it was much cleaner than he had expected. Or at least it appeared that way in the dim light afforded by the candle that Amy held.

"So, why did you bring me here?" he asked.

"We're going to play a game," Amy said. "Come here."

Amy sat down in a clear spot on the floor, placing the candle in front of her. She motioned for him to sit.

Douglas felt apprehensive. He was not the kind of kid to sneak around and break into forbidden places. He was beginning to wonder if a game was being played on him. Was this some kind of prank? Was he here to be made a fool of by Amy and her friends?

But also, he was excited. He was excited to be with her. He was excited to be in this forbidden place. He was excited to find out what kind of game Amy wanted to play with him. He was excited by the idea that maybe this was not a joke and Amy actually did want to be in this place with him.

So, he sat. He looked across the candle sitting between them, watching the light flicker and play on her face. He was about to say something when she spoke.

"Truth or dare?" she said.

"Huh?" He felt his face go warm and flush.

"Truth or dare?" she repeated. "Haven't you ever played it?"

"Of course I have," he lied.

"Okay, then, you start."

He certainly did not want a dare. He did not want to have to do something stupid and embarrass himself in front of her right now.

"Truth," he said.

Amy grinned at him. "What's something bad you've done?"

"Okay, um, my, um... I cheated on the math test last week. I copied from Lilly. She sits in front of me and I could see her test. She's way smarter than me."

"Hah! That's awesome. Goody-goody Douglas cheated on a test!"

Douglas was ashamed at his revelation, but she did not seem to be judging or making fun of him. She seemed genuinely pleased with this answer. He smiled.

"Now you ask me," she said. "You say truth or dare."

"Okay, truth or dare?"

"Dare," she said. "What do you want to dare me?"

"Okay… um…" *Kiss me,* he thought. "Um, do a pushup," he said, not being able to think of anything remotely clever or interesting.

"That's the dumbest dare I've ever heard!" She laughed as she put her hands to the floor and did a single pushup.

Still laughing she said, "Okay, truth or dare?"

"Dare."

"Dare," she repeated. "Dare. I dare you to touch my face."

"Touch your face?" he asked. "Like, just touch it?"

"Yeah. With your fingers. Touch my cheek."

Douglas brought his hand up and put his fingers to her cheek. He moved them across, feeling the softness of her skin. Back and forth, savoring the sensation until she suddenly pulled back.

"Does it feel normal to you?" she said.

"Normal? Like, do you feel like a normal person?" he asked. "Yeah. I mean, it feels nice."

She smiled just a bit and said, "Now it's my turn. Ask me."

"Okay. Truth or dare."

"Truth," she said.

"Okay, same question for you. What's something bad you've done?"

There was a pause as she stared at him. Douglas, waiting for some revelation, some mystery or exciting morsel of knowledge, simply looked back at her expectantly.

"How much truth do you want?" she asked.

"Truth," he said. "I want all the truth. That's the name of the game, isn't it?"

"Okay. All the truth. Do you remember Jim Samson?"

"Yeah, of course. He was a good guy. We played basketball

together. It was messed up how he just disappeared. Really sad."

Douglas felt a weight settle on his chest. Jim had been his friend. Douglas had never known anyone who had died before, and he thought that Jim was probably dead. He hadn't been seen in over a year.

"It was me. I killed Jim Samson," Amy said.

"What? Shut up. You didn't kill anyone. That's not funny."

"I killed him," she said again, looking right into his eyes.

Douglas stared back. This was, of course, not at all where he wanted this adventure to go. He had thought he might get his first kiss. He had thought he might get a girlfriend. He had not thought of being a confessor or hearing the fate of his missing friend. These were not the truths he had in mind.

She continued. "I killed him, and I ate him."

This was too much.

His mind stalled on this. He became angry at this game. He pictured little Amy sitting at a table with parts of Jim Samson on a plate and a napkin neatly tucked under her chin.

"What do you mean you ate him?" Douglas nearly shrieked. "This is insane." He rose to his feet. "You are just messing with me now."

Now he was certain he was being pranked by Amy and her friends. He pictured Claudia Ansel, Anita Sanchez, and Lilly Ashton sitting outside listening, waiting for him to cry or scream or make a fool of himself.

"I'm out of here," he said angrily.

Douglas reached for the door and saw that it was blocked by a thick black branch. He stopped. He stared at the branch for a moment, unsure where it could have come from. It was the width of his wrist. Dark black, but glistening like it was wet. It crossed diagonally from near the top of the door to the bottom.

The branch writhed and swayed gently. It stretched from the bottom of the door, across the room toward Amy, and disappeared into the darkness, away from the candle's dim sphere. It seemed to move with her. When she swayed, the branch swayed as well. When she leaned in to speak, the branch leaned in.

"You can't go, Douglas," she said. "The game isn't done. You haven't heard all of my truth."

Tendrils sprang from behind her—smaller than the one baring the door but dozens of them. They whipped and thrashed the air as they grew.

Douglas stared, frozen with horror and indecision. He could not get through the door with the black arm barring it. He could not move toward Amy with the monstrous growth seeming to sprout from her back.

He looked frantically for another exit or a weapon. He spied the window with its spider web remnants. But as he willed his legs to run toward it, the tendrils shot forward. They encircled him, grabbing his shoulders and arms, wrapping them in black flesh that dug into him and made him scream. They jerked him toward Amy. They forced him to the floor and he found himself, again, sitting in front of her.

"I'm not bad, Douglas," she said. "I didn't want to kill him. I thought I could stop with Jim. I thought it would be okay after that. But I couldn't stop. That was a year ago. A whole year without eating. Can you imagine? I didn't mind so much at first, but the hunger kept growing and growing. I've gotten so hungry. I'm so empty. I need something now."

"But I've seen you eat," he protested. "We have lunch

together every day! I see you sitting with your friends, eating. I have watched you."

"You watch me at lunch. That's sweet! Yeah, I ate at school. I ate in front of my parents. I put food in my mouth and chewed and swallowed like I remembered. But it's not really eating. Not now. So, I took Jimmy. I took him right in this place. Where we are now."

"But I've known you since second grade!" he screamed. "You aren't some kind of monster. We were in the play together in fifth grade. We sat together in Art in seventh. I know you."

"That was fun. I remember the play. You were a sheep." She smiled. "But that wasn't me. Not me now. That was me, before. I wasn't always like this. I wasn't always hungry. Frances did this to me. Do you remember Frances Holland? He did this to me."

Douglas did remember him. Another kid who had simply gone missing three years ago. All the parents thought he was kidnapped or had run away. His family wasn't the greatest, so most people thought the latter. The police had looked for him, of course, but not too hard.

"Frances got me alone. He was exciting. I wanted to be alone with him. But I didn't know what he was. I didn't know he would give me this."

Amy paused. She looked down. Douglas, through his fear and revulsion, thought he saw sadness in her.

"Sometimes it happens like that. It goes to the next person. Frances got me alone and he ate me. He wrapped me up and it hurt. It hurt for a long time, but I woke up and I wasn't really me anymore. And he was gone. But it doesn't always happen like that. Sometime it is just me still and the other person is just gone. Like with Jim."

"You killed him. You killed Jim and you're going to kill me? Is that what you're going to do?"

"I don't know if it will happen to you or if it will just be me again who leaves this place tonight. I kind of hope it's you. I don't like it so much, how hungry I get, how I have to fake like I'm still me. It's hard."

Douglas felt the tendrils on his arms and shoulders tighten. As he stared at her, Amy seemed to be loosening. He could not think of another way to describe this. It was as if her form had become unpinned somehow. Her skin bulged and shimmered. Her body expanded and sagged. Her skin became gray, then darkened, then darkened more to match the black of the tendrils.

Douglas struggled to move from their grip. He arched his back and strained his legs, trying to stand. He watched as Amy's transformation completed, as she lost her form and become a black mass upon the floor. She was a writhing puddle of black. A thousand tendrils and offshoots coming from her, twisting and flailing at the air.

Her voice came from the form, but he could not see a mouth. "I'm sorry Douglas. I really am. I'm so sorry. I'm so hungry."

The black Amy mass moved closer. The tendrils holding his body pulled him toward her. As they met, he felt a shock. He felt cold. He felt as if his skin were peeling off. She was right. It hurt.

He tried to scream, but his mouth was full of blackness. The dim light of the candle disappeared. Then the pain disappeared. And soon after that, Douglas disappeared.

Amy awoke later that night in darkness. The candle was gone. Douglas was gone.

She rose and walked out the door of the shed and across the empty field toward the school.

Not this time, she thought.

A tear formed in her eye. She laughed. She did not know she could still cry. She wanted so badly to be done with this. She wanted to pass it along to someone else and be done with it. She wanted to disappear like Frances had and sleep or die or be nothing, whatever it is that comes after this. But tonight, she would go home again and hug her parents goodnight. Tomorrow she would go back to school. She would pretend all the things that need pretending.

As she strode across the field, she felt a small emptiness in her stomach. It felt tiny now, but she knew it would grow.

EDWARD MATTHEWS lives in Salt Lake City with his wife, 2 children, and an incredibly destructive hound dog. He toils away the day as a government cog, but when night falls he retires to the solitude of his loft to peck away at his computer. Although he has dabbled in writing fiction for some time, *Truth or Dare* is his first foray into publication.

BUT WHAT A SHEEP

BY A LYN BUNDY

The shouting from downstairs petered into anguished wails, then quiet crying. Brian wasn't interested; a much more engaging drama was unfolding on the tiny screen of his iPhone. Brian had spent months trying to lure new followers to his social media accounts. But he was an average kid in a boring family, living in a quiet neighborhood. He had less than thirty followers, meaning he was a complete loser, a nobody. Now, like manna from heaven, he had a chance to change that.

Brian's younger brother Michael, punishing a bad animal by trying to skin it was nothing new. His parents yelling, pleading, and calling Michael a devil was also old news. But this was the first time the animal had lived... and escaped. The first time anyone in his family had done anything interesting. Unfortunately for Michael, it was also the first time he'd used hot glue to close a cat's mouth to silence its rebellious cries or experimented with electricity.

Brian felt the eye of the world turn slowly toward him, staring out of the tiny screen, and he was enthralled. His most recent video, a quick skateboard ride around his block, had almost eight hundred views! His previously most popular video only had seventy-three. Even more exciting, he had two hundred new followers and thirty-five comments.

Had he seen the cat before?

Post more videos of the neighborhood!

Who had done it?

The people wanted him.

Mom and Dad emerged from the basement weary and scared. Mom went straight to her room to pray and Dad collapsed into his favorite chair.

Brian's chair rocked; he realized his body was bouncing. He tapped his fingers quickly on the tiny phone screen. The story of the living skinned cat had made national news. His eyes raced through angry comments, his heart pumping almost too quickly. He clicked on a commented link and gasped. Unable to contain his excitement any longer, he had to share.

"Look, Dad! There's a GoFundMe for the cat!"

"Not now, Brian!" Dad growled.

Brian scrolled quickly down the GoFundMe page. People from all over the world seemed to be donating toward the cat's medical expenses. "Woah! It's at five thousand! How many cats can you buy for five thousand dollars, Dad?"

"Brian! Not Now!"

An animal rights organization from California pledged $1,000. Brian could hardly believe it. The cat had been ugly and old before Michael had gotten his hands on it.

"Six thousand!" Brian shouted. A chill ran down his back and he turned quickly.

Dad's eyes were wild. It was the same cold, punishing look

that appeared on Michael's face whenever an animal was about to get it.

Brian escaped outside with a shiver. He looked back at the phone, his blood pounded through his body, screaming in his veins. This was the most exciting thing that had ever happened in his life. Did no one understand? There might be TV cameras. They might interview him! Maybe he should do a vlog.

His head was bursting with possibility. His chance was upon him and he could feel it slipping away already. He couldn't go back to being stupid, loser Brian with thirty followers; he needed to act now. His fingers started typing. "I know who did it."

His phone buzzed with a reply, then another. Brian held the buzzing phone with both hands. He turned up the sound and closed his eyes as it buzzed and dinged. His fingers hovered over the keys, his body vibrating. He needed another hit. His YouTube videos were small-time. With one comment, he had engaged the world.

"My little brother," he wrote, "skinned the cat alive."

In a matter of hours, he had thousands of replies. Some called him a liar. He almost threw the phone down, rage bubbling inside of him. He wouldn't tell them, then! If they didn't believe him, they didn't deserve to know.

He checked the GoFundMe page. "Eight thousand!" he whispered. He uploaded a picture.

The instant responses filled Brian with pride. He was growing more powerful. Finally, they were answering to him, watching him, looking for him. It wasn't long before someone in New Jersey had unearthed his location. Someone in California organized a bus. The internet was coming tonight.

————

THE LOCAL BISHOP was visiting Michael's family when the buses arrived. "He's not evil," the bishop assured, smiling at the boy. "Just a little lost sheep."

"But what a sheep." Dad muttered. As the adults talked, Brian wiggled his legs impatiently. He couldn't risk looking at his phone now and getting it taken away. Brian looked at his little brother instead. Michael seemed smaller than usual. He was hunched over on his chair, looking defeated.

"The cat bit Brian." Michael said hesitantly. "It was bad. A bad cat." His blue eyes were wet and pleading. Brian squirmed in his seat; he had never seen Michael look so unsure. Luckily, the adults started telling Michael about Hell again so Brian didn't have to say anything. He turned away slightly to not have to look at those sad eyes, trying to focus on the warm phone still buzzing in his pocket.

When the bishop finally opened the front door to leave, a growing noise from outside drew the family onto the porch. The street seemed full of angry people, their faces masked in hatred. There were more people here than he'd met in his whole life. It was intoxicating.

The slim girl who lived next door was standing on top of Mom's car. She had a loudspeaker and was chanting with the crowd, "Save the cat! Cage the boy! Save the cat! Cage the boy!"

Brian pushed Michael forward. "He's here! Right here!" Michael stumbled forward, nearly falling on the ground.

Mom and Dad froze by the door, clutching each other with their faces strangely absent, looking like a loading GIF.

The loudspeaker fell to the ground with a crunch and an

electronic shriek. The girl on the car was looking at her own phone with a hand up to her mouth.

Brian clenched his fists, seeing everyone's attention on the ugly girl. He couldn't even remember her name, she wasn't important.

The girl dropped her phone. She raised both hands to her lips. "It died! The cat died!" She screamed.

"Monster!" A rock sailed out from somewhere in the crowd. It didn't hit Michael but the crowd cheered. They were louder now.

Brian's face was hot, drunk with excitement. He wiped his sweaty palms on his jeans to check his phone. He already had it open to the GoFundMe page. They already knew about the cat's death. The comments were angry, demanding that the money be spent hunting down the killer. Brian stepped forward and began reading out the messages.

I'll give a thousand to the one who skins the filth!
He's not even human!

Brian screamed. The crowd roared in response. Pure power shook through him. He was controlling this living lava flow. He was Hell's own auctioneer. Brian pushed past the bishop, shoving people aside until he could retrieve the fallen loud-speaker.

"He's a psychopath" Brian screamed, punching the phone in the air for emphasis. "The GoFundMe hit fifteen grand!"

Michael turned toward Brian, looking confused.

Brian smiled; his little brother didn't understand how much money that was.

"Brian!" Michael was running toward him, reaching out for his big brother.

The crowd grew louder, shouting their righteous anger.

Someone grabbed Michael's arm. A red-haired woman marched right up to the boy, crowd trailing. "Let's pour hot glue in your eyes, you monster!" she screeched.

Mom finally seemed to shake awake and made her way through the crowd. "Brian! Stop!" Mom screamed. She grabbed the woman's hands. "Wait! He's a child! My baby! Stop!"

The woman went quiet. Her eyes were angry but she looked confused, unwilling. The mob roared behind them but those confronted directly by Mom seemed unable to follow through on their threats. Instead, miraculously, they pushed back against the crowd.

Brian dropped the loudspeaker, staring at his mother's quiet influence. But those who couldn't hear the mother's desperate pleas grew louder and more violent. The crowd pressed forward, trampling the hesitant. The circle bent, collapsed.

The bishop tried desperately to reach the center, shouting, "God, provide a ram!"

Brian's body hummed with the crowd's energy as his fingers flew across his phone, reporting the scene. *They've got him!* Brian typed, then switched to his phone's camera.

A man tripped next to him, knocking the phone out of his hands. Panicked, Brian dived where it fell. The crowd opened and Brian saw his brother lying too-still on the ground, his head red. Next to him was the phone.

Brian jumped into the chaos, stepping on arms and legs to reach it. Kneeling, he picked the phone up gingerly. White lightning cracks covered the once smooth black screen. The broken glass caught at his skin as he rubbed his thumb along the edge. Brian felt a sob in his chest. He looked at his brother's body lying still. A shock of dread ran through Brian and the phone dropped again. Brian closed his eyes and opened them again, seeing. Terrified, he stood, hearing the phone's screen shatter under his foot. He didn't care anymore. He turned, meeting every vacant, sheep-like eye, hating every face.

"You're killing him," Brian yelled. His desperate cry pierced through the cacophony of the crowd.

Somewhere behind him, his mother screamed.

A feminine voice in the back—that annoying neighbor again —trumpeted, "Holy Crow! Seventeen thousand! It all goes to whoever skins him like the cat!"

Brian reached for his brother.

The crowd surged forward.

A LYN BUNDY is a Utah native who graduated from Utah State University with a degree in Literature Studies (aka Reading). She lives in Riverton with a husband, five children, and way less chickens than she wants.

PART II

INTERMEZZO

TAKEN TO TAKING
BY FRANK VAZQUEZ III

Taken and torn
under the moon.
I too shall be taking soon.

Now, they're swarming
and I their feast;
with every bite I become a beast.

Where once were thoughts,
a silence screams,
drowning what were mortal dreams.

I rise again,
a stumbled pace,
your beating blood, my eternal chase.

FRANK VAZQUEZ III's first encounter with horror was with film. He can't remember the title, but the first scary movie he saw was set in space, where an alien attacked the crew of a spaceship with a three-clawed tentacle. He never saw that film again, but that one moment spawned his love for all things frightful. When able, he goes ghost hunting or watches horror films to satisfy his cravings for fear.

DARKNESS DWELLS

BY FRANK VAZQUEZ III

I am your night,
your vessel of fright,
consuming all with my crepuscular might.

My shadows you fight,
as you hunger for light,
are fuel for your fears, which brings such delight.

When the dawn comes and burns with its bright,
I'll always be lurking, though not within sight.
So do good deeds daily, before your last rite,
for tomorrow may be when your ashes ignite.

MONSTER'S FEAST

BY JOSHUA SORENSEN

While Trolls dream of supper,
The Ogres, flesh do rip.
Werewolves love human hearts,
And Vampires take a sip.

But there is one creature,
As Zombies oft complain,
That eats every morsel
In their gluttonous reign.

It is gruesome Maggot.
The youthful Lord of Flies.
Munches on your innards,
Comes squirming from your eyes.

Oft preferring dead flesh,
Consuming live meat, too.
And when you pass away,
They will come for you.

HARPY

BY JOSHUA SORENSEN

Sitting on a perch
Among the twisted trees
She uplifts her face
Into the summer breeze.
The wind rustles lightly,
Softly through her hair
She feels its sweet caress
That is beyond compare

For in her face is beauty;
A beauty so sublime
Her immortal body marks
Not the pass of time.
But such chimeric beauty
Is often a mixed lot
In younger days it was this
Beauty that was sought

But such a noted beauty
Is often envy's cause;
So in lieu of tiny feet,
She now has only claws
Great wings of feathers
Have sprouted from her back
And now an itching hunger,
Accentuates her lack.

When she speaks, a cackle
Is all that will come out.
Instead of shapely nose,
She has a beak for snout.
Her silky singing voice
Alone with luck was spared
And so she uses that
To capture prey unsnared

She calls out through the forest,
Beckoning to man
To them that hear, she murmurs:
"Love me if you can."
Her song they often hear
And swiftly they approach,
But when they see her face,
They suddenly reproach.

Thus rejected—jilted,
She answers hunger's call
And eats the heart and drinks of blood
Of suitors one and all.
And thus forever lonely,
She sits upon that limb
Dreaming of her one true love
And calling out to him.

MOTTEPHOBIA
BY C. H. LINDSAY

Turgid moon
Whitewashes night
In luminescent primer:

Exposes living souls
As shades of gray.

Ravenous
Horde hunts choice minds
Hidden within detritus.

Desiccates worm,
Caterpillar and toad.

Zombie Moths,
Unsated, rise;
Rage against uncaring light.

Endlessly crave
Unattainable life.

THE CLICKER-CLACK MAN

BY JODI L. MILNER

When the shadows loom right
At the darkest of night
And their fingers stretch long and thin,

Comes the Clicker-Clack Man
With a blade in his hands.
Do I dare to invite him in?

If I don't, he will scream;
His sharp teeth, they will gleam;
The feast moon will turn dark and red,

And the stars will go hide
When he eats me alive
And my blood, around me, will spread.

If I do, I am lost
For I can't pay the cost
When in he comes bearing a test;

It's far better to win
Than to give him my skin
And to keep my soul in my breast.

He insists on the game
And my wager — my name
With no choice, I play, and he cheats,

But I know my foe well,
I'm familiar with Hell
So I stall until dawn fills the streets

In this trap he is stuck
And I cling to my luck
With every keen throw of the dice

There is nothing to fear;
Precious daylight draws near.
He flees without claiming his price.

So please listen, my friend
When the night's at its end
And the candles are burning low,

Comes the Clicker-Clack Man
And you best have a plan —
Defeat him, or end up below.

JODI L. MILNER writes award-winning short stories and has a handful of fantasy novels in various stages of completion. She holds a leadership position in the League of Utah Writers and works to support and educate writers at all stages in the process. When not writing, she can be found folding children and feeding the laundry, occasionally in that order. She has worked professionally in both human and animal medicine. Find her online at jodilmilnerauthor.wordpress.com and on Twitter @JodiLMilner.

PART III

DIGESTIF

MOUTHWASH

BY JOSHUA P. SORENSEN

I put my toothbrush into its stand, gargle the rinse water, and spit. Leaning close into the mirror, I examine each and every of my glistening, white teeth. Then, just as precisely, I floss between them. Dental hygiene is important and my dentist always reminds me that flossing is a healthy part of that regimen. I know that a while back there was some big hoopla about there never having been a scientific study proving that flossing was important. But what the crap do they know? There has also never been a study that water hydrates you either.

I discard the used string in the trash next to the other strings, used toothpaste tubes, and empty plastic bottles. Swishing back and forth, I follow the entire procedure with minty-fresh, fluoride-added, gingivitis-killing mouthwash.

And who doesn't just love minty-fresh breath?

"Can't spend all night looking at our teeth."

Some people might find it insane that I talk to myself, but I'm the least crazy person I know.

My reflection stares back at me from the mirror. His hair lies across his head akimbo. Not too messy, just enough to pretend he doesn't care. A five o'clock shadow leaves the impression of ruggedness. Beards are in right now. And of course, my reflection is impeccably dressed.

"Are you ready to go clubbing, Bob?"

Most people name parts of their own anatomy. For me, my reflection has a name. He is Bob.

Bob looks awfully gaunt tonight. Pale, a bit wasted away. His cheeks and eyes look sunken. I would put on some blush to cover all that up, but I don't have any and Bob doesn't like wearing makeup.

"You haven't been eating well, Bob. Not been taking care of yourself proper."

Bob just shakes his head and tisks in disapproval.

"Well, don't you worry, good buddy. We'll pick up something to eat at the club. Take a bite out of that hunger."

I laugh. Bob laughs. A joke between the two of us. Everyone knows how unhealthy bar food can be.

The trip into town takes about twenty minutes. I like to vary which clubs I go to. I've never been to this one, down on the south side. "Jumper's on 20th". I don't know where it got that name, since it's on 22nd Street.

It's a medium-sized club, one floor playing house music, the other hosting old 80's and 90's pop. Tonight is a good night to be here. Quite a number of people have come out for the evening.

I worm my way through the crowd up to the bar. Leaning in to the bartender, "Give me a Shirley Temple."

He gives me a questioning look. Maybe he couldn't hear me over the music and the crowd. So I repeat myself. "One Shirley Temple, please."

Still a questioning look.

"A Shirley Temple. 7-Up and Grenadine."

"I know what a Shirley Temple is. People just don't order that very often."

"Shirley you are joking?" A broad smile spreading across my face.

He laughs. I laugh. He gets me my drink. The chuckling continues under my breath. Laughing is superb. It's one of my favorite things.

Nursing my drink, I lean back against the bar. I scan the club to find my particular niche. I turn back to Bob, staring at me from the glass behind the bar.

"It does appear that we've wandered into a gay bar."

I guess the term would be LGBT bar, or something of that vein, since there are women here as well. This is not the sort of club that I would normally frequent, so the exact vocabulary escapes me.

"It's ok, though. Every good dog likes sausages."

The soda burns my nostrils as I giggle mid-sip. I see Bob clutching his nose, a roar of laughter interrupted. The bartender gives me a look and moves on to his next customer. I guess this is just another private joke between Bob and me. I'm sure some people would find the comment insulting, but that's not really the reason we are laughing.

Setting my drink down, I put a coaster over the top. Just leaving one sitting on its own is a big mistake. All sorts of things could go wrong with it, but I'm confident it won't be a problem for me.

The dance floor summons me. I glide out there, enjoying the cathartic movements to the thumping beat of the music. The crowd presses in around me. I can smell the sweat and pheromones. The stale stench of tobacco and alcohol permeates from moist skin. My stomach growls in complaint.

The cavorting mass of people doesn't contain the right person for tonight's escapade. Leaving the floor, I head back to my waiting drink. There is a man sitting at the table. He's a big guy, well-muscled and bearded. As I sit opposite of him, he takes a sip of his beer and smiles at me.

"Hi, I'm Lance," I lie. No reason to let him know my real name.

"Jim," he replies.

Discarding the coaster, I pick up my drink. The smell of some contaminate tingles my nose. Jim has clearly drugged my soda. This guy is a predator of the worst kind. Call it hypocritical, but I can't stand people like this. He deserves a sudden and abrupt appointment with karma.

Smiling, I take swig of my drink. Jim smiles. Let's not disappoint him. I take another swallow. The drug tastes horrible. Its flavor would be undetectable to most people, but I'm not most people and it is nasty.

I've found the right person. Jim will do nicely.

I'm not particularly good at small talk. It's even worse with men. That's probably because I'm not actually gay. Luckily, powerful pheromones exude from my sweat glands. It is a rare person that can resist my raw animal magnetism.

It doesn't take much time or even skill to have Jim eating out of my hand. I lean in close, allowing our checks to brush.

"Let's get out of here," I tease. "How about your place?"

I'm playing right into his plan, or at least that is what he thinks. But I need to make sure that he is completely sold on the idea.

"I'm feeling a bit tipsy. Maybe you could drive," I say.

Jim takes the bait, hook, line, and sinker. Just a few minutes later, he is leading me to his car. I feign drunkenness, or at least the effects of the drug. My charade continues throughout the trip to Jim's apartment.

His place is in a nice area. It's a trendy single bedroom that overlooks a public park. Jim is brazen bringing me back to his place after drugging my drink. He is probably counting on actions going unreported or, worse yet, just overlooked by local authorities. A sort of semi-official ignorance that sadly happens, particularly in the queer community. His kind of predators are a plague—a plague that needs eradication.

"I'll be right back," I promise, wandering into the bedroom.

Jim must be suspicious by now. Luckily, my musk has had time to work its magic. The logic centers of his brain are over-loaded with raw sex drive.

Jim is in the kitchen when I come out stripped down to my underwear. He is cooking on the stove. Coming up behind him, I wrap my arms around his shoulders. I am sure he interprets it as affection, but really, I'm just rubbing more musk on him.

"I'm hungry." One of the first true things I've told him. "But first, we have other things to do."

He is so enamored that he forgets to take the pot off the flame. Without protest, he follows me blank-eyed back into the bedroom. Jim leans in for a kiss. I grab him roughly and fling him onto the bed. His surprised look tells me that he doesn't comprehend how a wiry guy like me could fling his bulk so easily. He needn't worry; it will all be revealed soon enough.

"You are a naughty man," I say, dropping my boxers so they fall to the floor.

He giggles.

"You tried to drug me," I say.

"What? What are you talking about?" he lies, feigning innocence.

"Don't try and deny it. I know you drugged my drink, but what you don't know is that it didn't work. Unfortunately, you will not score this evening. I hope you aren't too disappointed."

If he was disappointed now, I was about to aggravate that feeling even more. I started into my speech.

"There is no need to resist. I'm hungry. Hungry beyond your imagination. I just want you to know that I take little pleasure in what I am about to do."

My muscles stretch. My bones crack. I grow taller. I used to hate this part, it hurt so bad. Now it is almost comforting, like a morning run. Fur sprouts from my skin. My jaw extends, carrying my nostrils with it. Sharp teeth replace my flat human ones.

My senses intensify. I can smell Jim's fear. Eyes now enhanced, I can see the heat from his body. As my ears grow into long points, I can hear his heart rate accelerate.

Finally, my favorite part. A tail shoots from the bottom of my spine and sharp claws grow out of my hands and feet. I let out a bestial roar. The sound reverberates about the room.

Jim's surprise shifts to uncomprehending fright. This is expected. Most of the time, my prey has moments of panic. I let him convulse in his unthinking reactions. The fear hormones flowing through his bloodstream will increase the nutritional value, or so I've heard.

I watch as he scrambles to the side of the bed. Pulling open the drawer on his nightstand, he frantically searches through it. He won't find the intended item. The small, automatic pistol that he keeps there has already been removed. I took it out when I was undressing. I've made the mistake of not searching for weapons in the past, when I was young. I don't know if it takes silver to kill a werewolf, but a normal bullet sure hurts. Five shots to the chest, it didn't kill me, but it took weeks to heal fully. I won't make that mistake again.

Jim screams. I leap.

His struggles are feeble and brief. I bite his right shoulder, tearing his entire arm free. Blood spurts from the wound, splattering the room with red gore. I let him scream while I crush his arm bones in my jaws and swallow his flesh.

Snapping open his chest, I eat his entrails. The lean meat of his heart and vitamin-rich liver slide down my gullet. I eat until my belly swells. Somewhere in the process, Jim perishes. His body grows cold.

I pull back from the carnage that has spread all over the black, silk sheets. Now comes the part that I hate the most. I gag. The taste of alcohol and tobacco intermingled with the gore. Why couldn't this man eat healthier and take care of his body better? Dry heaves wrack my body. With great effort, I hold down my meal. I slide off the bed, shaking my muzzle to remove the gore clinging to my fur.

My claws clack on the bathroom tiles. My body shortens as I return to human form. I turn on the water and splash my face, cleaning the reddened muck from it. I retch into the sink.

Standing, back straight, Bob stares at me from the mirror. His face contorted in a clear look of disgust at what I've just done.

"Don't look at me that way, Bob."

He disappears when I open the medicine cabinet. I rummage through the shelves, bottles and toiletries spilling out. I grab the tube of toothpaste and squeeze its contents into my mouth. All of it. The entire tube. I chew the paste and spit it out into the sink. I grab Jim's half-empty bottle of mouthwash. Tearing it open, I take a mouthful, swish it about, and expel it in a foamy goo.

Closing the cabinet, Bob comes back. White bubbles cover his lower jaw. His face isn't as sunken as it was earlier in the evening. I spit again and wipe my face.

"Looking better already, Bob. I guess trying to subsist on just chicken isn't the healthiest of diets. Humans may be more nutritious, but that taste is more than I can handle."

I take another swig of the mouthwash, trying to cleanse my palate. I gag again—the green, medicinal fluid running down my chin. Glaring back at Bob, I spit frothy spittle at the mirror.

"Why does everything that is healthy for you have to taste so bad?"

I empty the last of the bottle into my mouth. After all, who doesn't just love minty-fresh breath?

THE HUNGER

BY K. SCOTT FORMAN

The room was dark and the air hard to breathe. It was hard to take in a full breath without retching. It was the mice that failed to escape after eating d-CON, their small bodies lying and dying somewhere out of reach in a wall or the back of a cabinet, putrefying, being eaten alive from the inside out, the stench of their death getting stronger as they withered away.

The smell reminded me of my childhood. Reminded me of the time the power and water were shut off for several days after a hurricane. With no clean water or power to keep things cool, my father's butcher shop came alive with the scents and ghosts of blood and bone and meat and fat. The coppery smell one might expect isn't a smell at all. It's a taste; the taste of fresh blood. A bitten tongue. Old blood, blood covered by decades of water and soap and bleach is not the copper of pennies. It is like a dragon's egg waiting for the heat and fire of destruction to hatch. When old blood makes its way out of the pores of walls and floors and cutting boards and freezers it brings Death.

My father was a dragon and the fire.

Sometimes Death and dragons take a while to visit. They are almost always preceded by sadness or loss, but more often than not, hate and fear. I hated the shop. I hated and feared my father. Everything was black to me—not a color or shade, but an emotion, a temperature, a feeling. My heart pulsed and cracked in blackness, leaking gloomy fluid into my soul. Shadows and shades became my friends, my thoughts and feelings murky in their depths, and the hunger I felt deeper still.

The first time I was really hungry, I just started eating. And eating and eating, until… I don't remember actually stopping, but I do remember being grabbed hard on the back of the neck, pulled to my feet, and the fire. My father's voice was a flame that blistered and peeled any self-worth away to the bone. When there was nothing left to burn, a beating followed.

He was always sorry after the fire went out. The embers evaporated any tears he might have shed. There were always questions: Why had I done it? What was I thinking? Do you know what you did?

Somewhere in the maelstrom of adolescence, around that day in the butcher shop, I saw a glimpse of the future and the past—a connection, clear and cold and nauseating.

I vomited.

My father held my head.

It was the only time I loved my father.

It felt like I puked forever. I wondered if there would be any enamel left on my teeth or flesh left in my throat after so much stomach acid had passed. That's the moment it all started, where my revelation of past and future flipped a switch and I began to think and look at things differently. I had to be careful. I had to keep my feelings and thoughts to myself. I had to hide and sneak and wait and plan. Night became my companion with

Shadow and Shade, the world would stop turning under her gossamer cloak, and I would be free—just she and they and me.

The twilight of morning only sustains my patience. I reflect, I revel, and I forget all the tears of my suppers that only wake on my taste buds.

When the change happens my insides feel like an empty room, vacated by the living, the human living. It is only dirt and dust, decay and disuse. Life is still going on in the dark, in a black, abandoned chamber, a dim derelict hotel room, or a dusky moss and vine-choked hospital room in a deserted mental hospital with nothing but the ambiance of insanity and Death to keep one company. From the subterranean depths of my soul a bitter smoke rises. It taints my vision, my thoughts, and pricks my tongue, the taste buds vacillating between sweet and savory.

I'm no lycanthrope or vampire, no brain deficient zombie, but I am a monster. What can I do? I was born this way?

I must eat.

Everyone has to eat, everyone and everything. The problem is I eat everything.

And everyone.

This is why I have you chained, why we are subterranean, why you can't leave.

Remember the smokehouse in the backyard? The game freezer? All for you, you and those who came before–or at least what's left of them–and those who will surely come after: didn't I tell you?

You're the main course.

K. SCOTT FORMAN is a writer, editor, and teacher. He is a member of the Horror Writers Association (HWA), has had several short stories and poems published, and hopes the Great American Novel is just around the next bend. He enjoys long walks with his dog, sunsets with blood in them, and Metallica at volumes determined unsafe by the Surgeon General. He resides in the Rocky Mountains with his wife, a son, and a collection of guitars.

AUDRA'S CONFESSION

BY JOHNNY WORTHEN

It was easy to fall in love with Winston Granger. He was gorgeous and lovely and shone like a warm sunrise on the movie screen. Lots of people loved him, but not like me. I sensed something deeper in him. Before I could name it, before I understood, I still knew it. Before I knew it, I still knew it. See?

I first saw him in *Rented Room*. It wasn't his first film, just the first one I saw. He was only a year out of acting school. New York and Los Angeles. He did both coasts—two years in each. Doesn't that show dedication and ambition? He made his success happen. You know he was born poor, right? Like me? From a dysfunctional family too, like me. He rose above it and made things happen.

He was my inspiration, my guide, my other half. Once I found the secret and understood him, there was really no other path I could have taken than the one I did. I regret nothing. Even now, here in isolation, I regret nothing.

In *Rented Room* Winston plays a college student named

Alvin Fairchild and he's the boy next door to Sharleen Cranston's character, Sue. Sue is a bitch and doesn't recognize how wonderful he is until the final act, but by then, Winston—I mean Alvin—realizes that another girl, the girl next door to him on the other side, is The One. Great twist, don't you think? Sue has nothing when her rich boyfriend dumps her for a debutant and my dreamboat has the love of his life.

I couldn't afford to see *Rented Room* more than two or three times, but I've re-watched it a million times in my head, replaying it night after night as I fall asleep, seeing Winston's face, hearing his friendly encouraging words. I played it on the bus between my ears to and from Mezzers grocery store where I helped in the back and sometimes stocked shelves until they fired me. I went on food stamps for a while after that and moved to a smaller place and then my car.

Winston went on to make six other movies where he showed that sensitive side of him that makes him so lovable. I know what you're thinking—he's an actor. Actors act. They're fakers, but you can't fake what he has, not like that. He wasn't acting— well, he was, but that inner glow isn't pretend. He was shining, not acting. Shining. And that glow makes him famous because it is so true and real.

I finally had to move back in with my folks. They had a little run-down apartment. Papa was on oxygen and still smoking. My mom spent her days stretching their social security checks to the end of the month. I was looking for another job every day and helping as I could. Papa wasn't very happy about me coming back.

"Audra," he said. "You've been a disappointment your whole life. Now you're a burden."

"Sorry, Papa."

"It was your mom that let you come here. Her, not me."

"I know, Papa."

"You need to thank her."

"I will, Papa."

"You know we don't have a lot of money. Cigarettes aren't free. You need to get a job. A good job. Bring in some money instead of taking it out. You don't see your brother being a burden on the family."

Bryce had moved away right out of high school. We didn't hear from him much. He keeps away.

"I'll get a job, Papa, and I'm really thankful for all you're doing for me."

And I was thankful. I couldn't do anything out of my car. I couldn't even buy gas. I couldn't keep my clothes clean or my hair washed and combed. It wasn't easy. You don't know. You can't get a job if you look like you need one.

But luckily after that, it was only a couple of weeks later that I got a job. A good one. I was a filer at a doctor's office. They used paper because the doctor was old and didn't like computers all that much. I got to know the alphabet so good that I could tell you in a second which letter came before another. Not after it, but before. See? That's the trick. I can say the alphabet backwards now. Really fast, as fast as I can say it forward.

But back home Papa still wasn't super pleased. I didn't make much money and I was still big. Well, fat, and that really bothered him.

"You look like that Star Wars guy," he'd say after a few beers.

Mama would be at the table with scissors and coupons, the TV on too loud. Sports and beer commercials.

"I know, Papa."

"What was his name?"

"Jabba."

"No the one that looked like a big fat slimy slug."

"Jabba the Hutt, Papa."

It was around then that I stopped eating so much. I was told at work that my size was making my job harder. I think it was just a nurse trying to be encouraging about a lifestyle change, but I took it to mean they would fire me.

That was the first time I knew hunger.

There was no diet plan. I just didn't eat for a while. Then I didn't eat much. I read an article in the doctor's waiting room about fasting and health and I did that, but what they called fasting, I pushed to hunger. Hunger is different.

Most people don't know hunger. Strange that I didn't until I did it to myself. Mama had always put food on the table. Even in the darkest and poorest moments—Papa passed out on the couch, the bill collectors at the door—Mama would find macaroni or a can of tuna. Chips, lots of chips, and cookies. And sometimes pastries, day olds and discounted, but sweeter than her eyes.

"You eat up, girl," she'd say in a whisper in the kitchen. "Please. It makes me happy to see you eat. It means I'm…"

Funny thing is, she said that to me when I was little and again when I moved back. The exact words even. I never found out what came after "It means I'm…"

Mama died with Papa in a fire last year. It was big, took down the whole building. Luckily only those two were killed. They say it was started in their apartment in the living room by a cigarette and was fed by Papa's oxygen tank. Mama always said it would happen. She might have made it happen. I don't know. I wasn't there. I hope she didn't. I hate to think of the terrible fate she would suffer for that—hell and judgment. It would be worse than here.

But hunger, yeah. I learned it. I know what it is.

When you stop eating, the first things to object are your habits. When you're used to having a candy bar on the bus and you don't get one, your hands get fidgety and your mind wonders *what's up?* It's surprising how much habit there is in eating. It's a ritual and it's soothing. Drop that and you're up for stress, I can tell you.

After that comes the tummy rumblings when food is not there. If you're always eating, as I was, it'll come on gradual. If you have a schedule of eating, like I do now, it'll come on like clockwork. The rumblings last a while. They get stronger and weaker throughout the day for the first days. That's the physical hunger part. It hurts, but it goes away. It might take a day or two but it goes away and then there's elation. It's like drugs. A euphoria. I think this is what the mystics talk about during long fasts. It comes after three days for me, sometimes four or five, then it goes away.

Weakness is always present during hunger but sets in for real after about a week. About ten days was all I could do. You gotta eat. There are some things you just need and can only go so long without. Food is one of them.

I couldn't go hungry in front of Mama when she was alive. I made up friends and told her I was going out with them. Papa then got mad, saying I was wasting money, so I changed my story to visiting a girlfriend across town for movies on TV and leftovers. When I gave Papa my paycheck—just signed it over —he took it and bought a bottle of gin. It made him happy.

Mama noticed the change sure enough. She asked about it

and I said the doctor had put me on a pill to help my weight. I didn't like lying to Mama, but I did it. Papa yelled from the front room that maybe I could get some pills for Mama, though I didn't see why she'd need them. She was beautiful as she was. I liked her big hips and bosom, her rosy cheeks. My parents were quite a pair really, Papa was thin, he had the lucky metabolism that Bryce got. Mom was always a little round—not bad, not bad at all, but still a full-figured gal, if you know what I mean. When Papa would get drunk sometimes he'd say a beanpole married a pumpkin. Growing up, I liked that, since pumpkins were my favorite thing about autumn.

My biggest challenge became clothes. I grew out of my old ones and had to get new ones. I was afraid to use my money to buy them, Papa by then was used to getting my monthly check for household expenses. Mama took me to a second-hand store and we decked me out pretty good for cheap. I found a long flowery dress that looked just like Angie Young's dress in *Clocktime*, one of Winston's greatest roles. A movie I'd wanted to see so badly that I actually cashed my check and took the movie cost out of it before giving it to Papa.

Winston Granger was so lovely in that one. He was again cast as the nice boy—the only role that he truly inhabited. He'd made that stupid *Countdown to Mars* the year before where he was the villainous scientist. He was good in that, talented, but you could tell he wasn't comfortable doing it.

Anyway, I loved that dress I got with Mama, and though it was light and casual, I only wore it out on special occasions. Sometimes, I'd put in on at home in my room with the washing machine running and the rain seeping in under the window and I'd imagine I was the Angie Young's character in *Clocktime* going back in time to meet Winston Granger under Big Ben, finally understanding the subtle cues of his love and kissing him with all my soul. And him kissing back.

After I lost the weight, I got a raise. I was thin then, really thin. Maybe too thin. I'd completely gone the other direction. The nurse started talking to me about eating disorders and support groups but then would complement me on how good I looked. Sometimes I even thought I saw the male techs looking at me in *that* way, but nothing ever came of it. I was making other plans.

I kept hungry. The feeling in my stomach and mind still hurt, but it became like a star. A bright burning star. It became part of me. It never went away. I couldn't pass by the office donuts or smell my mom's spaghetti without the stirring gnawing pain like a living—or maybe a dying—thing. It hurt. And I let it. No other way to say it. It hurt and became part of me until the hurt was what I had, who I was. The hunger.

One day I passed out at work and woke up in the break room. I said something about a cold and they let me go home early. I didn't go home though, I sat in my car at the park and thought about things. I couldn't let it go, I realized. The hunger was driving me. It was a fuel and I needed to use it, but I had to recognize the limits.

I went and got a big piece of chocolate cake and ate half of it before throwing it up in a gas station toilet. It was good though, and broke the hunger. I ate "normally" after that. I stopped losing weight and didn't faint at work again.

I figured it out, see? Hunger drives you. It points the way to happiness and makes you get what you need or kills you in the attempt. No wishy-washiness. Get it or die. Keep trying until you can't any more, and then keep trying some more, see? There's a spiritual component. Your whole soul gets wrapped up in it. A physical need transferred to a spiritual necessity. All of your being wrapped up in feeding the hunger. Because you need it. You can't survive without it. No one can. Hunger and want will drive you to get what you need because, well, because you need it. The trick is to realize when you have it and accept the win. That's what that cake was. My win. I fasted only, like, every three days then and let myself have a treat at least once a month.

I learned to take in the floral dress so it still fit me, and then I got an idea.

It was bad of me, but I didn't tell Mama or Papa about my next raise. Instead, I had them transfer it directly into a bank account no one knew I had and issue me a check for my old amount. I'm sure the office manager wondered why, but he didn't ask.

That was how I got the money to move to California in only a year.

I'd tried to write Winston letters. I even sent one, but never heard back. That was okay. I knew he never actually got it. He would have responded had he seen it, because I knew.

You see, I knew the hunger in Winston's eyes, which are the lenses to his heart. He played the roles that spoke to him, to his needs, and I knew I had the same ones. We were yin and yang. I saw it in every performance he did. I read it between the lines on his webpage, in the cruel tabloid rumors, in his Twitter feed and award speeches. I knew he was looking for something and I knew I had it.

Maybe there could have been someone else for each of us, but why wait? You see, all though my life, he'd been there beside me, he—by whatever name or movie—was my friend, my confidant, and my lover. Yes, I said lover. Lover means more than just sex. But love is wonderful. Mama loved me and I loved Winston Granger. He is my lover. That's how it is.

And this is where they say I'm crazy, but I know what I know and see things and know things and feel things. Hunger is a knot, an emptiness that needs filling at any cost. Any cost. I know it and I sensed it in Winston.

My biggest worry was that when he met me, saw me, knew what I brought him and accepted it, he'd lose his acting career. His hunger, like mine, would be satiated. He'd no longer be able to be that on screen. And that kept me away for a while, but then I remembered that a quest must have an ending. His hunger had served him as it should by bringing me to him. I would be his food, his nourishment, and he would be mine.

Of course, I was arrested the first couple times I tried to see him. I went to the wrong house once, scared a kid on a trampoline. Another time I got onto a movie set and stayed behind a big backdrop until I heard someone call his name. Security was on me before I even saw him. The last time I was arrested, the third time they slapped a restraining order against me. That was humiliating—not for the order, I didn't care about that, but I'd expected Winston to be in the courtroom and had worn my floral dress and done my hair and my eyes just right. My heart was ready for him to see me, to recognize me. I knew he had only to look at me and he'd know. But he didn't show. He sent a lawyer and somebody from his agency and I got a fine that sapped most of my money and a stern talking-to by a bald judge.

I thought about the agency guy being there. I was on my third day of fasting and all was made clear. Winston was too popular and important to be let free. They'd keep him from me, they'd keep him hungry because they were using him. They were taking his checks to pay themselves. Buying houses and yachts and gin. I realized that even when we got together and completed each other, they'd work against us and break us up. We'd have a few hours, or weeks, or years maybe, but they'd beat him down with insults and derision and claim he'd never work again if I was around.

And he might not.

He'd miss the hunger because it was part of him and drove him. I knew that. He'd have to toss me aside eventually to recover it. I understood that finally. And my love might tell me to let it happen but my experience with hunger would fight it. Remember the win part? Knowing when you've succeeded, when you have what you want, it's not easy to see when starvation is driving you. Starvation removes much of the higher thinking. Want and drive are all you know. You could eat yourself to death given a chance. Look at how you get sick if you're thirsty, really thirsty, and drink too much water. Things are short-circuited. You could also eat and then go the other way to never being satisfied again, because you don't recognize the goal is right in front of you. Right there. Like that time at the premier with me in the audience listening to Winston take questions—not mine, but some good ones about his method and funny outtakes that'll be on the DVD. I was right in front of him and he didn't see me. He couldn't. The hunger had him.

I went to his house and climbed the wall late one night when no one was there. I'd planned it like a thief—brought my stuff in a black bag and knew when the patrol car would pass by. I timed them with my watch and no one stopped me. It was very cool and to be clear here, I could never have climbed the fence had I not lost the weight. It all made sense, see?

I figured the house was alarmed so I waited in the bushes

with a bagel, well, half a bagel and a packet of margarine. It was the next day, around one in the afternoon or so, when I heard his car pull up. He parked in the driveway and went inside. I gave him a few minutes to turn off the alarm and then broke a window in the study at the back of the house and let myself in.

When he didn't appear from having heard the broken glass, I figured I was safe.

I put on my dress and fixed my hair and eyes and lips. I'd remembered to bring a mirror so it wasn't so hard.

I heard him upstairs shuffling around and I went out into the foyer. It was grand. I knew that he'd bought the house and fixed it up and that it'd once been owned by some silent movie star who built it during his heyday. The parties they used to have there were the talk of the town, and the gossip.

I stood at the bottom of a white marble stairway on white marble tiles, admiring the wooden banister and modern art. The sad lines of the paintings told me again of Winston's loneliness and hunger, and a tear rolled down my cheek knowing that I was about to end that.

"Winston," I said. Then louder, "Winston, come down. I'm here."

It got quiet. Then I heard footsteps.

I waited and glowed. I felt the power in me and wanted Winston to see it.

He appeared as if out of a dream atop the stairs. He was dressed in leather pants and a tee shirt, real rock-and-rolly. He had a tattoo on his bicep and looked like he hadn't slept all night. I figured he had a new role, a bad-guy biker coming to terms with his tender side and he'd had a long night shoot.

He glanced around the entry looking for danger but only found me.

"Who are you?" he said, leaning over the railing.

"I'm Audra," I said. "I bring what you hunger for."

He was amused, I could tell, that little sly smile that hid such depths of longing curling the side of his sweet mouth. He looked at my dress, whether he recognized it or not, I don't know, but I could tell he liked it.

"Do you now?" he said in an intimate way.

I know what you're thinking. He thought I was a prostitute or a fan wanting a romp. He might have thought that, but deep inside we both know that I brought him more than that. I could have slept with him, given him my flower. I was long overdue for that, but there was no use. That would have fed a sexual hunger, but like I said, I was there for greater things.

"Come down," I said. "I'm here."

He looked around again and stood straight. He hiked up his pants and then calmly, slowly, intentionally, rounded the platform and moved down the stairs. He had cowboy boots on, black and leather, like his squeaking pants. He kept his eyes on me and I felt a sexual feeling I did not know or under-stand. I melted in his eyes—the lens to his soul, and shuddered.

"Audra is it?"

"Yes. I'm Audra."

He smiled and I felt my knees weaken. But I kept strong. Driven by hunger, his and mine, I stayed strong.

I did not wait for him to come all the way down. I knew if he got too close, he'd stop me. His nobility would allow nothing less. His goodness would outshine his need.

I drew the scalpel from my bag. They'd not miss it. It was never used. It was some old keepsake from the last century.

Seeing the silver blade, Winston paused.

"For you." I held my hands out to him to show him the gift in my right hand, handle toward him. "For us," I said.

I'd practiced. I found the spot beneath my breast and pushed the blade between my ribs. It was harder than I thought it would be, but I was strong and I drove it in with a luscious slurp and gasp.

I stood there and smiled at him, but Winston did not understand. That was alright. He didn't need to consciously know. I was working in other areas than that.

How does one fill a spiritual hunger? Can a solid hunger be sated by a gas? Can food calm a soul? Heck no. That's not how it works.

His face went white. A tear of happiness streaked down my cheek.

He could save me. I was not dead. He had only to come down and carefully, lovingly, take me to the hospital and I would be saved. Unless I removed the blade, which I did.

Immediately my dress spread with blood. Hot, surging life spilled out of me but I kept my eyes on my love and let my joyous tears fall to my breasts in little splashing drops like the rain in *Rented Room.*

"Oh my god," Winston said, and then, as was his kindness, he rushed forward.

I fell into his arms.

"What are you doing?" he shrieked.

"Feeding you," I said.

And I pulled him close. And I kissed him. I held his lips to mine, I tasted him. I felt his heat. He let me. See? He let me. It was meant to be.

I opened my eyes and looked into his, to his soul. Still kissing, I held the air in my racing chest, feeling it burn me, and mix with me and absorb all that was there, until it was my fire, my heat, my very soul. Then I breathed my last breath into his mouth and tasted my blood on his tongue.

Happy in his arms, in his breath, in his eyes, I died.

I knew doing this would hurt him on some level, but I also think I saved him on another. I don't know this. I don't know as much as I thought I would here, in this dark and quiet place. It is a different kind of loneliness than I knew before though, not so bad. I have Winston. I feel him. Alone in the dark, waiting, I feel him and I am glad. Satiated. I'm in him. We are together. I think one day I'll be able to leave here, but I'm in no hurry. I wouldn't leave now if I could. I wouldn't. Not now. I need to be here to fill that need in Winston the way it is finally filled in me.

He will never forget me. He cannot remove me. We are complete.

JOHNNY WORTHEN is an award winning best-selling tie-dye wearing author of books and stories. Trained in theatre and standup comedy, he has graduate degrees in modern literary criticism and cultural studies. When not teaching, Johnny writes upmarket multi-genre fiction—thriller, horror, young adult, comedy and mystery so far. "I write what I like to read," he says. "That guarantees me at least one fan."

FEASTY-FEAST

BY MICHAEL DARLING

Dinner. Not hard to get. Not hard at all. Just reruns.

Brains not fulfilling. Not anymore. Not since Pala almost died.

No. Not since.

Full-filling. Yes. Food in tummy-tum.

Fulfilling? No. Food always reruns now. Bland. Boring. Bad.

Ingk regarded his prey.

Stupey-Stupe. Sits all day. Tiny screen. Big screen. No different. Stupey-Stupe watching crappy-crap.

Ingk stuck out his tongue.

Blech.

No choice. Need to keep tummy-tum full. Need to keep pretty-pretty Pala alive for another day. Poor Pala. Broken wing. No fly.

No hunt.

Ingk flexcd his fingers. Twitched his wings. Flew.

Zip.

To the ear of Stupey-Stupe. Past the little hairs. No touch. Over the skin. No touch.

No repeat Pala's mistake.

Through the canal. Stop at the membrane.

Up.

Through the hole he had drilled in the bone. To the brain of Stupey-Stupe.

Dark.

Ingk's light slits glowed. Brighty-bright.

Dinner. Many pits and scoops in Stupey-Stupe's brains. Many dinners eaten.

All reruns.

Ingk sighed. Dinners were fulfilling before. Dinners taken from *her*.

From Feasty-Feast.

Feasty-Feast had been good dinners. Delicious. Full of many tasty things.

Feasty-Feast had also been quick. Pala's mistake. Bad flying. Touched the skin. Touched the hairs. Feasty-Feast so quick with her hand. Her finger poking in her ear.

Pala's wing broken. Ingk had pulled Pala farther in. Into the canal. Safe place near the membrane. Heart pounding. Eyes weeping. Waiting. Feasty-Feast finally falling asleep. Ingk carrying Pala back. Back to the hovel in the wall. Barely able to fly with Pala in his arms. Barely getting home.

No dinner.

Not that night.

Only crying.

Ingk had been angry. Had wanted to go back. Back up the hole. Tear up Feasty-Feast's brain. Rip. Tear. Scoop. Squish.

Waste.

Couldn't go. Had to care for pretty-pretty Pala.

Feasty-Feast left next day. Out the white door. No coming back.

Since then, only Stupey-Stupe brains.

Ingk went to work. Scoop from here. Scoop from there.

Stupey-Stupe never miss it.

Blood pooling at Ingk's feet. Walking back carrying pinky-pinks. Bloody footprints through the bone tunnel. By the membrane, licking the blood off feet. No trace outside that way. Through the canal.

Light slits off.

Out. Flying away.

Stupey-Stupe moving his finger across the small screen. Staring at the crappy-crap. Absently scratching at his ear.

Too late. No broken wing for Ingk. Ha ha.

Ingk flying. To their hovel. Zip. Through the hole he had drilled in the concrete wall.

Pretty-pretty Pala waiting. Her eyes gray. Broken wing. Sad —but pretending.

Ingk let Pala pick a pinky-pink. Watched to make sure she ate. Keep the tummy-tum full. She closed her eyes after each bite. Ten bites. Tiny bites. Licked her fingers even though it was for show. Gave Ingk a small smile. Pretty-pretty smile.

Satisfied, Ingk ate. Big bite.

Closed his eyes.

Emoji of poop. Rerun.

Text: "what r u doing?" Answer: "tv." Text: "me 2." Another rerun.

Images: red cars. Sneakers. Girls in bikinis.

Reruns. Reruns. Reruns.

No fresh. No tasty.

No meaning.

Ingk's bites all the same things. Same crappy-crap. He didn't bother to close his eyes. No new tastes. No reason to bother. No reason to watch/see.

Full-filling. Yes.

Fulfilling. No.

Ingk plopped down. Sat in the dust. Traced a picture. Maybe make Pala smile again.

Pointed nose. Tail fins. Jagged fire. Porthole.

Pala pointed. She knew Ingk's favorite. Her high voice: "*Martian Chronicles*. Tasty dinners."

Ingk nodded. Drew again. New spot. Ocean waves. Curve of land. Palm tree.

Pala waited. Too many good dinners. Could be a man on the beach. *Robinson Crusoe*. Could be a box under the tree. *Treasure Island*.

Ingk added a boat with a big cat.

"*Life of Pi*." Pala clapped her hands, making Ingk smile. "Yummy-yum."

Pala fluttered her wings. Happy. Then winced. Pain.

Ingk saw Pala start to cry. Ran his fingers through the dust to erase the drawings.

Stupey-Stupe dinners not fulfilling. Not helping Pala get better. Not helping her heal.

Not for a moontime.

If Pala keeps not getting better . . . no. Not good thinking.

Ingk made fake yawn. Pretending to be tired. "Nighty-night?"

Pala nodded. Pala always tired now.

Ingk stood. Took Pala by the hand. Walked to their little bed. Cotton-ball mattress and dryer sheet blanket. Settled in.

Pala snuggling into Ingk's shoulder, eyes wet. Ingk careful to keep hands away from Pala's broken wing. Let light slits glow softly. Keep away the dark.

Ingk prayed no bad dreams.

Slam. Stomp.

Ingk's eyes opened.

Good prayer answered. Morning now. No bad dreams.

Ingk slip out of bed. Look at Pala. So small. Gray. Broken.

Voices. Knew voice and new voice.

?

Sneak through wall. Wings itchy-twitchy.

Stupey-Stupe on the couch already. Tiny screen in hand. Big screen on too.

Reruns.

Then.

Bouncy-bounce. Girl with red hair. Jumping. Skipping. To the couch.

Stupey-Stupe not noticing. Playing with screen.

Girl with something. Not screen.

Ingk saw. Watched Girl open the something.

"Don't you have a phone?" Stupey-Stupe noticed. Finally.

"This is better." Girl showed Stupey-Stupe. Pages open.

"Whatev."

A drop of water landed on Ingk's foot. Water-not-water. Water-drool.

Ingk swiped the saliva off his lips.

Feasty-Feast had read those things too. Before going out the white door.

Impulsive. Ingk took off. Flew over the Girl and her book. Memorized the words. Back home. Zip.

In the hovel, in the dust, Ingk drew the words.

Pala would wake up soon. Ingk would show her the words.

The Adventures of Tom Sawyer.

Ingk stepped back. More drool falling. Tonight, he would fly.

Hunt.

Pinky-pink and blood. Fulfilling. Healing Pala.

Feasty-Feast again.

MICHAEL DARLING is the award-winning author of The Behindbeyond series. The first novel, *Got Luck*, hit #1 on Amazon. Michael shares his hole in the wall with his wife, pretty-pretty Shauna, two Ingks and a Pala. Three of Michael's short stories have previously been published in this anthology series.

tioners of the dark arts, and zombies will haunt every corner of your mind as you read these thrilling accounts of what could happen during the end of days in Utah.

Reanimated corpses of religious fanatics proclaiming salvation are the least of your worries...

The Great Salt Lake is a remnant of an ancient lake that was almost as long as the State of Utah. What mysteries does it hold in its briny waters? What secrets lurk in its murky shores?

…a malevolent spirit haunts a pregnant woman, luring her ever closer to the salty depths, yet what it wants is much more horrifying than death…

…the inversion and smog in the Salt Lake Valley carries more than just bad air…

…two locals find more than they bargain for when they unearth an ancient box buried in the salt-caked muck…

…a trip to Wendover turns deadly when *something* decides to tag along for the ride…

…a young girl hears voices in her head, voices that keep her company. But there's something else in the void of her psyche, something that's growing stronger, something that wants out…

Whether its mystery, apparitions, ancient curses, or a

modern day apocalypse, one thing holds all these tales together: The Great Salt Lake. Nestled inside the second anthology of Utah horror, are tales intended to delight a wide range of readers, everything from traditional horror, to romance, comedy and young adult. The authors share a connection to Utah (bringing them closer to the salty depths of the lake) bringing the reader another taste of local talent ranging from the "salty" veteran to the slick greenhorn. Sit back, cuddle up in a warm blanket, and stay away from the water while you enjoy these tales from the Great Salt Lake.

The West has always been a symbol of the wild frontier, rugged adventure, and dangerous exploration. However, if it wasn't for fear of the unknown, the West would just be another cardinal direction. Old Scratch and Owl Hoots delves into that fear and captures it in fourteen tales of terror set in the West ranging from the 1800s to the present day. Take a gander inside and you'll find stories dealing with…

…a strange creature on Antelope Island that can never satisfy its hunger…

…a young girl kidnapped by highwaymen; but she carries a dangerous secret…

…a woman's vacation to Zion National Park that takes a dark turn when she can't stop hearing the cries of a newborn baby…

…an outlaw on the run from Porter Rockwell who finds more than he bargains for in the Utah wilderness…

…a war veteran who carries a darkness inside him that threatens his very own family.

Experience these stories and more in Old Scratch and Owl Hoots. All the stories in the anthology are written by authors with Utah connections. Some are veterans at the craft, while others are making their debut. Cozy up next to a campfire and delve into these fourteen stories and find out why it's dangerous to be out and about in the West when the sun goes down.

ARE YOU A HORROR WRITER?

This anthology is brought to you in cooperation with the Utah Chapter of the Horror Writers Association.

For information on joining the Horror Writers Association, please visit www.horror.org.

If you are in Northern Utah and would like to meet up with the Utah Horror Writers, please visit their Facebook page for news and updates about meetings and special events: www.facebook.com/UtahHorrorWriters

www.ingramcontent.com/pod-product-compliance
Lightning Source LLC
Chambersburg PA
CBHW070436120726
47910CB00003B/812